I0709490

WHITE FLAGS

Jo Marr

MEDIA TEAM LOGIC, INC.

White Flags

Copyright © 2023 Media Team Logic, Inc.

All rights reserved.

No part of this publication may be reproduced, distributed, or transmitted in any form or by any means, including photocopying, recording, or other electronic or mechanical methods, without the prior written permission of the publisher, except as permitted by U.S. and Canadian copyright law.

For more information or permission requests, contact:

whiteflagsnovel@gmail.com

The story, all names, characters, and incidents portrayed in this production are fictitious. No identification with actual persons (living or deceased), places, buildings, and products is intended or should be inferred.

Book Cover by Jolyon Meldrum

First edition August 2023 Canada

ISBN - Ebook: 978-1-7380538-1-0

ISBN - Paperback: 978-1-7380538-0-3

ISBN – Hardcover: 978-7380538-2-7

ISBN - Audio: 978-1-7380538-3-4

First Edition: August 2023

To my parents,

Zaki & Jeanette

Forward

I have always wanted to write a book. Most of you who read this may have also dreamed of someday writing a book. It's a lovely daydream but in reality, it's hard work, plain and simple. Many years of dedicated and disciplined writing, writing, and rewriting. Why did I write this book? Let's start by saying it was never meant to be a book in the first place.

As a filmmaker, I always imagined it as a feature-length film. A movie that would entertain and move people in a way some of the classics have for their sheer power, inspiration, and magnitude in their capacity to celebrate the human spirit. In fact, I had written the screenplay first, and that in itself took many years. But when I realized this was a script that was challenging to make in the traditional sense, I realized it may be a while...or may never get made at all. There are many factors that decide when, why, and even if a film should get made and this one had all the odds against it. However, I strongly believed in the story and its message so I was determined to make it available in any form I could.

Hence, I decided to adapt it into a book. The process is usually the other way around, a book is made into a film. But I was never one to conform so here we are. To my absolute surprise, the process made each better; the book made the screenplay better, and vice versa. Now to be clear, the first few drafts were pretty, how shall we put it, not my best work. I learned quickly that writing a screenplay and writing a book are two completely different skill sets.

I was experienced and solid in one, but not so much in the other. Fortunately, I had the help of a gifted writer, Rowen Woods, a dear friend and trusted editor, who so passionately supported my efforts and deftly and with kindness showed me how awful my initial work was.

Some of the other feedback, or blowback, you could call it, was the question of why me? Why am I telling this story? What gives me the right? I have often asked myself the same question. Why me? The easy answer is, why not me? But it's a little bit more complicated than that.

I am a huge fan of human stories. Stories about real people that say and do real things. And this is a story that came together as a result of my collective experiences, education and frankly, my insatiable curiosity. I wanted to tell a story that would stay with you for a long time. Just like some of the novels we read in school, those characters have come to be people we know and loved or hated. But we remember them as if they were real people. And they were, to us. I want to humanize humans as if they were friends. That is how I hope to treat characters I write about. How can I handle it the best way I can?

I hope one day this book will be used in schools and book clubs to inspire discussions. I chose to tell this story in a part of the world that is both hugely volatile and widely misunderstood. It has a complicated history and like all history, is often skewed in the direction of whoever benefits from whomever is telling it. But there is no history lesson or contextual background in this story. There is no lecture. Just what I hope is a powerful, gripping story.

So, is it a hot topic? That would be an understatement. It's such a divisive topic that depending on which side you are perceived to be on, could amount to losing your friends, family, career, and in some extreme cases, your life. That is not what I wish upon anyone. That is not the point of this tale. In fact, the opposite. I hope this book brings people together in a way that is real and productive with meaningful dialogue.

I decided to tell my story around a region steeped in a violent history but I also made it more palpable with a fabled vision of what I could imagine it being one day. I use the word fabled because in today's world, this story unfolding the way it does, and how it concludes, could be considered someone's naïve fantasy. But my question is; Why does it have to be a fable? Why can't it happen for real? In real time? In real life?

I hope you enjoy this enough to recommend the book to others whom you believe would also appreciate a good read.

Chapter 1

The explosion was devastating. Things that could move moved. Things that could not were blown apart — torn and shredded into jagged chunks transforming them into a rainfall of dusty debris. For any person standing nearby, it was hopeless. As they lay dazed, streams of blood flowed while desperate thoughts of home merged with final breaths that gradually expelled into the sulfur-fueled air.

Minutes earlier, Reservist Major Benjamin Shani was relieved. The cavity that had been growing louder every day had just been filled. As he shifted into second gear, his phone rang. The voice on the other end was unmistakable; he had known it since they were old enough to kick a football around in the settlement where they grew up.

"You drove right by me! You didn't see me?" Moshe was a master of playful accusations.

"Where are you?"

"Turn around! I'm in front of the bookstore across from the dentist."

"Ok, ok. I'm coming back!"

Excited, Shani was about to crank the steering wheel when... *BOOM!* His world changed forever.

He felt the explosion first and then heard it echo through his phone in an eerie delay. He adjusted his rear-view mirror to see a billowing cloud of smoke and debris rising above the rooftops. Wrenching the wheel, he rammed his foot down hard on the gas pedal spinning around in a haze of sand and dirt. Oncoming traffic immediately stopped for him as they would any military vehicle that was hurried. Only one scenario ran through his mind as he raced along the narrow streets, weaving in and out of the congested cars with their alarmed passengers pointing at the smoke —a suicide bomber. He immediately knew the brash sound of a homemade bomb barely absorbed by the perpetrator's body as it tore outwards through everything around it. The only question was... how many people did it kill?

When he arrived at the bookstore, or what was left of it, it didn't take long for him to locate his friend's broken body beneath a layer of rubble —the phone still clasped in Moshe's dead hand —the signal still strong — *the call still live.*

News of the bombing traveled quickly. Mobile phones began ringing everywhere emanating from the bodies of the dead and dying. A cacophony of ring tones collided with one another —pop song melodies fusing into a discordant symphony of panic: mothers calling sons; fathers calling daughters; husbands calling wives... wondering, "Are you still alive?"

Shani rose and took in all of the devastation as the sound of sirens filled the air. This was now personal. He would lead the investigation. He would have to mourn later.

Thousands of kilometers away, Doctor Rami Amar was perspiring through an uneasy sleep in his Bucharest office. His persistent nightmare had returned.

The butt of a rifle smashes into a young man's face, his blood splattering against a concrete wall. A light bulb swings, casting him in light, then shadow. The man's eyes are hollow. He screams in raspy, urgent bursts...

Startled awake, Rami took a moment to reorient himself and realized the *urgent bursts* were issuing from his phone. He snatched it up and held it to his ear. The voice on the other end was shrill and overwrought.

"It's all your fault! It's all your fault!"

Lyda —his wife's pain was instantly his as he listened to her breath scratching against her throat. He pinched the bridge of his nose trying to squeeze the fog out of his head so that he could respond, when a calm baritone abruptly cut off Lyda's voice.

"Rami, my brother, you must come home. It's Hassan. Something has happened."

Rami withered back into his chair, his stomach contorting into a knot.

"Do you hear me?"

"Yes, Marwan," Rami managed. "I'm on my way."

But he wasn't on his way. He was frozen —the phone still clenched in his hand. Only when the dial tone sounded errant was he reminded to put it back on its rocker.

He looked down at his wrinkled suit and tried to press it out with his palms to no effect. He rubbed his tired face and instantly his spectacles fell into his hands. He set them down and continued to massage his forehead. His hazel eyes were wide open now, adjusting to the fluorescent lighting and the late-day sun reflecting off the windows across the street. He stood and his tall frame creaked, feeling all forty-six years, as he attempted to push back his nausea.

He moved slowly to the window and stared down at the people below. Bucharest was alive —the world continuing on despite the phone call. His heart fluttered then steadied into a deep, mournful pounding. He'd prayed he would never get this call —the ache in her shrill rebuke —his brother's-somber tone. Returning to his desk, he turned on his computer to check the news. *Suicide bomber kills 30, injures hundreds.* Rami slumped back into his chair. His instincts were confirmed —his heart knew it —his soul knew it. He drew a breath in and then breathed it out slowly and loudly, but the answer was still the same. His son was dead. Shattered and numb, he made plans to return home.

Chapter 2

The heat was unforgiving, typical of Jordan in mid-summer. This was an unrelenting desert with rocky outcrops and intermittent remnants of shrubbery —the space that you had to get through to go somewhere else. The winds whipped up often leaving dust drifts painted across the road. A pale-yellow plume hung in the air as the bus Rami had managed to catch made its way towards the border crossing into the West Bank.

With its air conditioner broken, the vehicle had become a furnace leaving little room for comfort despite the open windows. Regardless, a toddler who had left his mother's side had taken to running up and down the aisle for the excitement of it all. This annoyed many of the already irritated passengers, but for Rami, it was a welcome distraction as he saw in the boy Hassan at that age —wide-eyed and eager. He leaned forward and offered the child a smile.

"It's fun, isn't it? But be careful!" Rami was surprised by the thinness of his voice, barely audible over the hum of the engine and the wind whistling through the windows. The boy ignored him and kept running. Now everyone was trying to coax him into settling down. Rami looked at the other passengers. A piece of Hassan lived in every face.

As the bus crawled along a winding section of road, the older woman who had parked herself beside Rami drifted in and out of sleep. She had dark circles under her eyes and smelled vaguely of oregano —her thick thighs pressing into his, each time the bus turned a corner. At first, Rami shifted away from her staring numbly out of the window at the parched landscape, letting the sweltering temperature and rocking motion of the bus lure his mind away to somewhere else — anywhere else. But after a while, he realized that he didn't mind the contact and his legs relaxed. The woman was familiar to him now, and he hadn't touched another, or been touched, in a very long time.

Exhausted, he leaned back and closed his eyes. His journey had already been too drawn out: complications with his booking on a last-minute flight from Bucharest to Amman; difficulties with security and customs; and mechanical problems with the plane —the list was endless. Each delay tingled beneath his skin like the warning signs of an oncoming virus.

Although Rami was a member of *Doctors with Wings*, it wasn't a license for easy travel. Being Palestinian, he couldn't land in Tel Aviv. Instead, he was forced to make his way to the West Bank through Jordan and deal with the same scrutiny and headaches as everyone else. That's just the way it was.

His mind fluttered back to the onset of his career. He had become involved with *Doctors* not long after completing his internship. Growing up in such a volatile region had infused him with the desire to study medicine —the ideal discipline to help alleviate at least some of the suffering he had witnessed. Then, the organization offered to take him to other areas where he could make a difference —Iraq and Afghanistan. It was a perfect marriage for a man imbued with both talent and empathy. Despite the danger, he never looked at it as risking his own life but rather as improving the lives of others. He was aware that this perspective helped keep fear at bay. It was also pacifying to know that after each tour of duty, he was able to return to his family and home —Beit Jbal —*House of Hills* —the small village where he'd spent most of his life.

In this existence, he'd felt content. There was plenty of work for a doctor in his village whether people could afford to pay for it or not. At the same time, he could be there for his loved ones. It was not an easy path but his life had meaning. That is until the night he was forced to abandon everything and everyone he cared for. *That night* haunted him still, prickling at him now as he opened his eyes and dabbed the sweat from his brow with his white cotton handkerchief.

As the bus continued to crawl, its gears grinding, his mind felt as exposed and shriveled as the landscape. He attempted to push the memory of *that night* far from his mind and stared out at the midday sky. The bus's tires continued to kick up wafts of dust, which ballooned and thinned as shafts of light danced on each particle of grit before settling. The effect was mesmerizing, inducing him to remain somewhere between his new home and his old, somewhere between calm and upset, between the comfort of sleep and being startled awake with every sudden bump in the road.

Rami knew the pain of being startled awake too well. He had been startled awake in the middle of the night countless times in Beit Jbal. He had been startled awake on *that night*. Even amid exhaustion, the memory refused to lay still.

When the bus reached a plateau, young boys playing football moved their game off the road to let it pass. They stood by watching with wonder etched on their faces. *Who are the passengers? Where are they going? Maybe one day I will go somewhere too.* Rami's eyes settled on one face in particular — an older boy of eleven or twelve who peered back at him with a smile dimpling his round, tanned cheeks. For an instant, there was a connection. *Such innocence,* Rami thought. There was nothing more moving to him than the openhearted curiosity of youth. He felt the warm swell of regret rise up through his chest. It lingered for a moment but then just as quickly faded. The boy waved but by the time Rami took this in it was too late to wave back.

Somewhere between another incoherent dream and one final nudge of his neighbor's thigh, the bus lurched and came to an abrupt halt. They had finally reached the border. Rami readied his passport and disembarked anticipating a long wait. Looking out at the wind-swept and arid land that ran from Jordan into the West Bank so harmoniously, he wondered at the absurdity of erecting walls and borders —killing and imprisoning others in the names of ownership and vengeance —the unending cycle of fear and hate.

He entered the terminal and a sudden eruption of giggles drew his eyes back to the toddler who had now settled himself on his mother's hip as she waited at a booth. The child was fascinated with an Israeli border officer who stood nearby collecting passports, his ears wiggling each time his jaw clenched. The officer looked up at the toddler's delighted face, smiled, and then resumed his duties. Rami shook his head in wonder. *Children*, he thought, *are the emissaries of hope.*

After hours of waiting and questions, Rami finally made it through the terminal. Once outside, he found a group of taxis waiting close by. From here, he would have to convince one of the drivers to take him the rest of the way home. He knew the driver would be happy for the business, though he would pretend not to be so that he could continue to negotiate the fare. It was always that way here.

Rami finally settled on a driver who looked familiar —a middle-aged man with a road map of deep crevices running across his cheeks and brow. The driver's thick dark eyebrows raised as Rami approached. Throwing down the butt of his cigarette, he grabbed Rami's bags and opened the taxi door.

Rami was glad to slide into the back seat out of the sun even though everything smelled of stale tobacco.

"Where to?" Asked the driver.

"Beit Jbal."

The driver's eyebrows rose again. "I can take you as far as the checkpoint. You must have heard of the bombings. They're interrogating everyone entering and leaving."

"I understand."

Rami turned and looked out of the window in time to see the mother with her toddler climbing into another taxi a few cars down. *Bombings*... he thought numbly ...*women and children being blown apart.* The driver hit the gas pedal as Rami closed his eyes.

Chapter 3

"One more passenger would double my income today," stated the driver after an hour of driving in silence.

Rami's eyes startled open. "I'll pay you double if you resist picking up anyone else until we reach the checkpoint." He was overheated and groggy and desperately wanted to be alone. The taxi driver shrugged as they passed a few scattered people walking along the roadside. He pulled a cigarette out from his breast pocket and flicked his lighter.

"Tell me, when was the last time you saw a doctor?" Rami asked.

The driver's eyes searched his passenger's face in the rearview mirror. "It's been some time. I heard they were coming around in a caravan so I went a few years ago."

"You were having chest pains?"

The driver looked surprised. "How did you know?"

Rami waved his hands in front of his face playfully fanning the smoke. The driver acknowledged his cigarette with a tilt of his head. "Yes. He told me to quit back then. I should have listened." A moment of silence drifted between them.

"Lung cancer," Rami finally said.

The driver nodded ruefully. For the rest of the journey, each man remained deep in his thoughts.

By late afternoon, they'd arrived at the barricaded checkpoint nearest Beit Jbal. "I can get out here," Rami stated as the taxi slowed to make way for a group of travelers. Nodding, the driver pulled over. Rami handed him the money they had settled on.

"How did you know?" The driver asked again as his passenger gathered his things.

"You have a scar on your chest in the shape of a horseshoe —the result of a mule kick from when you were a boy."

The driver was dumbfounded. Rami dragged his bags across the seat and slid out of the car. He looked over at the long line of people waiting at the checkpoint and then walked around to the driver's open window.

"I was the doctor in the caravan."

The driver's eyes widened and he shook his head in wonder. Rami tipped him a little extra, picked up his small suitcase, and then studied the mesh of barbed wire and cement blocks separating him from his village. He began walking forward as the driver, still shaking his head, drove away.

It wasn't long before Rami found himself beside the security arm that blocked all vehicles from passing. Anyone could easily duck under the arm and walk along the road, but being shot on sight was an effective deterrent. The checkpoint had been quickly erected as a result of a suicide bomber long before Hassan. It was believed the previous bomber was also from the village, so a special task force had been assigned to the area. Now that Hassan had been identified, the Israelis were able to mobilize quickly —ready to search, investigate, and interrogate —anything to get them closer to the cell recruiting the young and disenfranchised.

Rami studied the custom-built bunker —a concrete vantage point several meters down the road. A breeze appeared from nowhere and cooled his forehead gently as he contemplated his next move.

The small crowd that had gathered at the crossing milled about with no sense of order. Most of the stranded travelers were weary and frustrated; some slept on their luggage, while others fussed with their papers or waved anxiously at the guards attempting to get their attention. All had been waiting for hours to cross. This had been their way of life for too long and their irritation never seemed to diminish.

Outside the bunker, Israeli soldiers stood at ease quietly chatting, seemingly ignoring the crowd, but their eyes were trained to notice every nuance —every potential risk in the restless group awaiting passage. Rami watched quietly as a jeep rolled into view and a single figure exited. The soldiers instantly saluted. Even from a distance, the man's bearing radiated authority.

When Major Shani arrived at the barrier it was much to the surprise of the border guards even though they knew it was not far from the settlement where he lived. Shani felt that he owed it to Moshe to be there, and so he lit a cigarette and waited patiently next to his jeep. Lifting a foot onto the ledge of the open door, he rested his arm on his knee. He was tired from not sleeping well and his eyes felt gritty and heavy. He drew on his cigarette and immediately felt the guilt of becoming a full-fledged smoker again —something he'd promised his wife and girls he would never do.

He took another long drag as his thoughts drifted back to the day of the bombing. He had been thinking about Moshe for weeks and had intended to call him, but Moshe had called *him* instead. *It's funny how that works*, he thought as he inhaled the smoke into his lungs. He loved Moshe like a brother —he'd even introduced him to others as his brother — so when he'd found him twisted and torn on the ground, he was determined to find those responsible and eliminate them.

When he'd first approached his supervisors about heading the investigation, they sensed his desperation and refused, even when he assured them that he would be useless at his desk. Still, he persisted until they eventually agreed, specifying that he must follow protocol without exception. He calmed himself and nodded, but in his heart, he was unsure of how faithful he would be to procedure when confronting those who'd taken so many lives. *How severe could the punishment be for killing suspected terrorists, anyway?*

As the days rolled on, he did his best to dispel those notions and focus on the investigation as impartially as he could. He explained his new task to his wife knowing she would have misgivings. She could always sense the split in her husband —his desire for revenge wrestling with his professionalism —jostling for position. It was obvious that she wasn't certain which side would emerge victorious. *If darkness prevails*, Shani thought, *I will keep it from her and our girls. It is better this way.*

He took a deep breath and allowed his heavy, round shoulders to relax. He was a sturdy man in a compact frame, not defined by sinewy lines of muscle, but as strong as a wrecking ball. His throat was sore and the back of his neck felt tight, so he rubbed out the knot where his neck met his shoulders. When he grimaced from the pain, the contour of his skull was revealed beneath his skin. Once youthful wisps of hair, now mottled with grey, poked out from under his helmet and stuck to his forehead. He removed the helmet and rested it on his knee glad to feel the mildest breeze cool him. It seemed like only moments ago he was enjoying ice cream with his daughters, and now he was waiting for the man whose son was responsible for the murder of Moshe. *The father of my enemy is also my enemy*, he thought, stamping out his cigarette.

Down the road, Rami had given up on waiting. The soldiers would have to understand that these were special circumstances and allow him through. As he bent beneath the security arm, a hand instantly grasped his shoulder.

"They will shoot you!" stated a young man, his intense gray eyes wide with fear. He appeared to be in his late twenties, with the tanned brow and weathered cheeks of an old farmer.

Rami stared at the calloused hand gripping him and then slowly raised his eyes to its concerned owner who quickly released him. "This is my business, my friend," he replied quietly.

Uncertain, the young man stepped back as Rami reached into his bag and pulled out a vest decorated with a large red cross. He held it up indicating to the soldiers he was a medic, and then continued under the security arm towards them. The soldiers instantly formed a defensive phalanx and aimed their weapons.

"Stop, or we'll shoot!" barked the head of the unit. "Who are you and what business do you have here?"

Rami stopped. "I am a doctor, and I need to get through!"

"Drop the bags and open your jacket!"

Rami did as he was told.

"Keep it open and turn around slowly".

When Rami was fully turned and facing the soldiers again, he let his jacket flaps drop.

"Now walk forward, slowly."

Rami obeyed. The soldiers formed a semi-circle around him with their leader at the center.

"Give me your papers!"

Slowly pulling his papers from his pocket using only his fingertips, he handed over his traveling documents.

The unit's corporal studied them carefully, appearing unimpressed. "Why are you carrying

Romanian Residency when you are Palestinian?" He pronounced Palestinian as if he were spitting.

"I teach at the School of Medicine in Bucharest."

"What do you teach? How to get killed from foolishness?"

Rami raised an eyebrow. The young corporal was tall and swarthy with piercing blue eyes and cheeks scarred by acne. "Am I going to be killed by *your* foolishness, son?"

The corporal's jaw clenched as a dozen rifles slammed into the 'ready arms' position. Rami thought it might be the last sound he would ever hear when a squat figure stepped into the circle.

"At ease, Corporal Cohen!" Major Shani took the papers from the corporal's hands and gave them a passing glance. "Dr. Amar. I've been waiting for you." Corporal Cohen and his soldiers quickly made eye contact with their superior now fully understanding the purpose of his visit. The Major moved in closer. "Hassan was your son."

Rami showed no emotion. He knew there would be an investigation but he presumed it would be later in his home, with his wife. He was hoping to have some time to do his own investigating to find out who had influenced Hassan. Was he forced? Threatened?

Shani regarded Rami's cool demeanor. "You'd never know you'd just lost your only child." He puffed on his cigarette as he circled the doctor, taking him in. It made no real sense to him, but he blamed the man in front of him for Moshe's death. He could feel the hatred bubble up into his throat and nostrils like thick, infected mucus. His green eyes flared as he felt the power of his position surge within him —the power of life and death granted to him by the soldiers under his command — young men with guns who had his back no matter what.

Coming around full circle, he stood face to face with Rami and blew his last puff of smoke into his face. "You do not grieve because you believe in what he did?"

Although Rami was taller than Shani, the contrast in their postures made the doctor appear smaller. Shani stood straight —his chest high and dominant; while Rami's shoulders curved inward — heavy from his travels and grief. Rami felt the weight of Shani's power pressing on him. He knew that the major could have him killed in an instant, and he didn't want to die —at least not yet. "We all grieve in our own way," he answered, an air of defiance coloring his tone.

Shani flinched. This man in front of him was not entirely what he'd expected. He shoved the travel documents into his breast pocket. "I will hold on to these. You're not permitted to travel outside this town. And if we determine a curfew is warranted, you will not defy it or else you will suffer the consequences." He pulled another cigarette from its packet and lit it. "Someone will come to your house to speak to you further, perhaps me, but we will oblige you your son's funeral first." Turning abruptly, he marched towards the bunker. "Let him pass!" he ordered over his shoulder.

The soldiers did as they were told, watching Rami suspiciously as he retrieved his bags and walked away.

The natural descent of the road made for an easy walk home. Rami could almost let the momentum take him the rest of the way. The sun was losing its intensity behind the limestone hills, and the onset of an evening breeze was a welcome respite. Patches of greenery spotted the landscape where life fought its way through the dull beige rocks.

Most of the agriculture in the region required irrigation to survive, and it did so bountifully. Terraced plains supporting eggplant farms dotted the outskirts of the village, while the sharp scent of citrus from the lemon trees that lined the tracts of land, drifted along the lower hill. With them, the fragrant bloom of bougainvillea flared out boldly, clinging to the walls and gates that surrounded the homes along the road.

Rami breathed in deeply and released some of his fatigue into the scented air. He could see the narrow streets of his village at the bottom of the hill. The maze of white homes with their flat roofs looked untouched since he'd left —the odd carob, olive, and palm trees testaments that life continued despite oppression and conflict.

Tiny shops surrounded the fountain in the center square —the only source of fresh water for many. How many times had Rami taken Hassan to that fountain when he was a child and told him of its history? Surprisingly, this remembrance did not fill Rami with sadness, but with the sweetness of nostalgia instead; Hassan had been such an inquisitive child —always asking questions — always eager to learn.

Rami's eyes lifted to one of the hills where the now-defunct school sat. He'd had such hopes for Hassan at that school. He'd attended it himself as a boy, dreaming of the day he would leave to travel the world. There, Miss Noor Malouf —his favorite teacher —had managed to imbue him with both drive and confidence. His heart still swelled at the thought of her.

Miss Malouf was attractive in the way that every boy secretly admired, with sharp features, high cheekbones, and slightly concave cheeks that added ruggedness to her beauty. She was both resilient and charming and she knew it —like so many of the women in the region. She also knew how to engage the class and gave everyone ample time to express themselves. But when she called upon Rami, she would challenge him a little harder —smile a little broader —before moving on. Even after these many years, he still felt there had been something between them.

He pondered the withering of a place that had once brought him such a sense of worth and belonging. From where he stood now, the school looked like a rotting carcass —bullet-pocked and bruised with obscene graffiti. Rami ached as he took in its battered exterior. How he'd wished Hassan had received the same education he had so long ago.

He recalled how his son would often return home with a bloody nose or torn textbooks —the conflict and unrest among Palestinian youths steadily increasing as services became more limited and qualified teachers fled the country. It all came to a head when some of the more radical students shot and killed three farmers from a nearby Jewish settlement. The Israeli soldiers marched in, took the boys, collectively punished their families, and shut down the school indefinitely. Hassan was only twelve at the time.

Rami had tried his best to continue Hassan's education. He'd shared his knowledge of science and medicine, and improvised history and geography lessons with books from the small library near his office, but his work would inevitably call him away. As he looked down at the now empty building that had once housed the library, he recalled how, upon each return visit from some faraway country, he had found Hassan older than his years —more distant. *Still, he was a good boy... wasn't he? How could he be gone forever?*

When Rami finally arrived in town, dusk had settled. The center was surprisingly alive given that this was a suicide bomber's home. *Why had the Israeli Defense Forces not imposed a curfew?* Rami tried to wrap his mind around the IDF's unclear reasoning; like *collective punishment*, many of their actions only seemed to ensure more desperation and hostility.

As he neared his house, he could see candlelight flickering from within. The curtains swayed gently in the evening breeze and the people inside cast marionette-like shadows on the walls. Taking a deep breath, he slowly opened the front door, stepped inside, and froze. He felt too small and unprepared to face all of the relatives and friends who had gathered to offer comfort and condolences.

The house looked less spacious than he remembered but then there had never been so many people crammed into it before. Breathing in the aroma of beeswax candles and the tart stench of sweat from too many in too small a place, Rami pushed himself to move and set down his bags. No one noticed. His breath became labored and erratic. He reached a hand out to steady himself and felt the cool strength of the walls — walls he had built himself brick by brick.

As bodies mingled and moved about, a space opened up leading Rami's eyes to his wife. She was sitting in the center of the room dressed in black — tissues balled up in her lap and hands — with a group of women surrounding her. She was almost unrecognizable —her eyes swollen — with red welts marring her smooth cheeks. Next to her, a large photo of Hassan sat on an easel encircled by candles and flowers.

A sharp ache pierced Rami's heart. He felt Lyda's pain even more than his own, making their loss suddenly all too real. His love for her called out from every pore. "Lyda…" he whispered.

Mustering up his remaining strength, he was about to make his way over when a hand rested on his arm. The broad, tear-stained face of his brother greeted him. "How could this be? How could this be?" Marwan cried, staring into his brother's eyes. His hair was peppered with more gray than Rami remembered —his cheeks carved with deeper lines.

Rami had no answer. What could he say? He knew nothing, understood nothing. He pointed to Lyda and rasped, "Thank you."

Marwan engulfed him in a warm embrace. "Of course, my brother! Go to her!"

The exchange caught the attention of others who rose from their seats offering subdued expressions and indecipherable whispers of condolences as Rami made his way through the room to his wife. She was staring at the floor lost in her thoughts, her eyes weighted by the tragedy. As the crowd parted, she sensed her husband's approach and turned to Hassan's photograph.

"Look, my sweet boy. Look who has come to see you!" Bitterness colored her tone. "Look who has come all the way from…" her voice trailed off into a whisper. "…It's your father."

Rami knelt beside her and took her clenched hand in his attempt to make eye contact, but she pulled away. Her message was clear; he was a betrayer, a deserter, and an intruder. His abrupt departure had left a gaping hole in her life —in Hassan's life. Rami's reasons may have been valid —necessary for their survival even — yet still, she had felt abandoned. What was worse, Hassan had also felt abandoned, and, for that, Rami knew she would never forgive him.

Lyda rocked back and forth, her fists remaining tightly closed on the tissues that were twisted around her knuckles turning them white. Finally, she rose and walked out of the room leaving Rami on his knees wondering if he could ever make amends.

He raised his eyes to his son's smiling photograph. The flickering candles seemed to bring the image to life, making Hassan's eyes dance. His eyes were always the warmest part of him —rich, chocolaty-brown gems —shy, but also alert and friendly. Who could sway his son so far off course? In Rami's mind, Hassan could never bring harm to anyone.

Weariness finally overtaking him, Rami flopped into Lyda's chair unable to acknowledge those watching him. Out of respect, everyone slowly made their way home. Staring at Hassan's image, Rami shook his head in bewilderment. "This was not how we raised you," he muttered quietly; and the question *why?* tapped on his skull once more before his eyelids flickered and gradually succumbed to sleep.

Chapter 4

As dawn crept through the open windows, Rami stirred from his seated position. The house lay silent, everyone gone, and the candles had dissolved into pools of hardened wax. Feeling a presence beside him, he turned to find his son's eyes staring back at him from the photo. Without the flickering candles, Hassan's eyes no longer danced, but warmth still emanated from his thoughtful gaze. Rami couldn't bear looking at him and turned away.

A sudden clattering of dishes spilled out from the kitchen. Lyda was making tea. Rami slowly pushed up from the chair. His joints were stiff and the nerves in the back of his neck pinched. He massaged the long night from his aching body, stretched, and solemnly made his way to the bathroom. He needed time before facing her again.

Opening the bathroom door, he looked around. Nothing had changed but everything was different. Time had worn through the once-white tiles, which were now yellow and dull like the teeth of a smoker. The shower curtain had gone, turning the entire bathroom into the shower; and when a musty smell quickly found his nostrils, his eyes darted to the drain in the middle of the floor. The pipes running under the house were too old —too damaged; one more thing he had no control over, nor the energy to fix.

As he waited for the water to run warm, he gazed at his image in the small, tarnished mirror above the sink. Its warped center made his face appear distorted and unnatural. Beyond that, he looked gaunt —his eyes sunken and smoky. He bent over and splashed the soothing water over his face and neck, and then returned to his reflection. The water had changed nothing; the man staring back at him was someone he no longer recognized —an abstract portrait —raw and broken.

His hand reached to the towel rack and landed on his favorite towel. It was old and worn but he found its thinning scratchiness comforting. Lyda had chastised him for keeping it —threatened to throw the ancient artifact out a million times. Yet, here it was cleaned and ironed and awaiting his arrival. Rubbing it against his cheeks, an ember of hope returned his thoughts to her as he breathed in the towel's soft fragrance. She always added rosewater to her laundry. She knew he loved this.

His mind escaped to the past —the day he'd met Lyda at his brother's wedding. Beautiful women had surrounded her but to Rami, Lyda was the most striking —tall and slender with a dimple over her full lips whenever she smiled. They had studied each other through sideward glances. Then, when he'd clumsily spilled coffee on the pristine tablecloth, she laughed and whispered to her friend, her oval-shaped eyes soaking him in. How he longed to return to that day.

In the kitchen, Lyda rested her head on her folded arms at the table. The tea sat waiting on the counter, its sweet odor infusing the room with mint. Rami stepped towards his wife. He could see that her eyes were open and staring vacantly at the wall. Not wanting to impose, he sat down across from her and waited.

For a long time, nothing was said between them until Lyda finally managed, "The funeral is tomorrow," her voice cracking.

Rami nodded, his eyes following her as she mechanically rose to pour him some tea. He watched her move to the counter as gracefully as ever, her black dress clinging to her delicate frame. Even with her back to him, he could tell that she was exhausted —an invisible weight pushing down on her shoulders — slowing her usually deliberate movements. Still, the length of her back and the narrowness of her waist and hips had always reminded him of a ballet dancer. She was one of those women who could eat anything and remain willowy, even when she was pregnant with Hassan. Rami acknowledged that he would never tire of looking at her. He loved every last follicle on her body, and it would always be this way. He longed to hold her face in his hands and kiss her, but he knew he would be rejected.

He received his cup gently from her hands and rocked it back and forth, cooling it with his breath. He needed to bide some time before asking her that one question which was sure to increase her resentment. *Have courage* he thought as he looked up into her dark eyes —so similar to Hassan's in shape and shade. He breathed in deeply and then expelled his breath allowing the question to escape.

"Did you know?"

Lyda looked at him as if he were a stranger —not someone she had been married to for over sixteen years. Rami shrank back, disquieted by the contempt in her eyes. Yes, their connection had been abruptly cut when he'd left —he knew this —felt its responsibility sitting on his shoulders like a sack of rocks — but they had loved one another passionately once had they not? They had spoken intimately about their lives and childhoods, their fears and hopes for the future; surely that meant something? Couldn't she understand that he ached to know how attuned she'd been to Hassan's slow descent?

Turning away silently, Lyda moved to the counter and opened a bag of sesame seed hard bread —the type dipped in tea until softened and then eaten. This had been Hassan's favorite breakfast for years.

So this is how it will be, Rami thought. He took a sip of his tea, but his lips puckered and he pushed it away suddenly feeling swindled. "This tea is bitter," he complained, immediately regretting it. Lyda stared out the window with her back to him, leaning on her knuckles, holding in her venom. Rami knew by heart the expression that accompanied such a stance —every line that etched her lovely face when she was enraged.

He remembered the first time he'd seen her angry. That was the day he knew he'd fallen in love. A debate over politics had turned into an argument when she'd defended what he considered to be an insignificant point. Her face had become suddenly inscrutable, then defiant. He noted that when Lyda believed in something, her eyes narrowed from ovals into sharp black diamonds, flashing intelligently as she spewed out facts to support her opinions. Often, she would-ambush him with her wry sense of humor — facetious observations springing out amongst the discourse, causing him to marvel at how quickly her mind worked. He'd always been enamored by her cleverness —her wit —acknowledging that, if her father were another man, she would have attended university to pursue and attain whatever degree she desired. But, that was another life. In this life, the loss of her only son was the most unbearable event she would ever experience —a betrayal that banished the playful and brilliant Lyda to the past.

She slammed her fist down on the sesame bread sending its tiny seeds scattering in all directions. Rami wished they could go back to the beginning. He would do things differently. He would move his bride to a safer place, travel with her, and see her pursue her dreams before they settled down to start a family.

He looked at her clenched fists and rigid body. She remained facing the small window where she had once tended wild thyme and rosemary on its wooden sill. He wanted to ask her again, *'Did you know?'* but instead opted to slip quietly out of the room —rage mingled with heartbreak was not something he could manage at this moment. He opened the front door, felt a warm breeze brush his cheek, and stepped out from the stifling atmosphere of their modest home into the new day.

Chapter 5

Moving in any direction would have been a welcome relief from the fragile atmosphere in his house, but Rami soon found himself kicking up dust along a familiar road. The sun was now shining and the early morning heat began to intensify burning the back of his neck.

The question he'd asked Lyda bounced around in his head, still searching for an answer. As he continued to walk, his resolve to find out the truth intensified; he would get to the bottom of what happened to his son if he had to overturn every stone in the valley, and he would begin by talking to the man who knew everything about everything in the village —his brother Marwan. Rami's pace quickened.

Marwan's place was not a café by Western standards as much as it was a kiosk with a makeshift patio protected by a striped pullout awning. Once he rolled up the steel door there was just enough room to set out a few plastic tables and chairs.

Inside, barely clinging to the grease-splattered walls, were two faded posters that Marwan had lazily held on to for years; one —a bowl of faded fruit; the other —a large lemon turned white from age. Beneath the lemon poster, a crude wooden shelf held a collection of ornate Narghila pipes; while against the opposite wall, a cluster of backgammon boards were piled high on a rickety table. Four padded stools hugged the narrow counter and an ancient refrigerator had been squeezed behind the counter into a corner. In the other corner, a black and white TV crackled with the intermittent signal from the wobbly antenna on the roof.

A plethora of hanging utensils and pots, a well-used hot plate, and a discolored sink made up the rest of the kitchen. This was a place where men would gather to smoke contentedly, sip coffee or tea, and talk over the top of one another while their dice clattered on the backgammon boards.

Rami stood at the entrance, wiped his brow with his handkerchief, and sat down on a flimsy patio chair. From behind the counter, Marwan motioned to him. "My Brother! You will be more comfortable over here on a cushioned seat."

The customers stopped their game and watched as Rami slowly rose and made his way over to a stool. When he turned to acknowledge them with a nod, they all wordlessly resumed their game. The atmosphere had suddenly become heavy and oppressive, making Rami believe that everyone else knew something he did not.

The fact that he had left Hassan and Lyda under his brother's watchful eye did not escape Rami. How much did Marwan know? New questions raced through his head as he took the seat closest to the fridge thinking somehow it would make him cooler. Marwan watched his younger brother but avoided his eyes.

"Please eat something. Let me make you my famous French omelet."

"Just a cola, brother."

Rami turned his gaze out into the street where two young boys were throwing rocks at an assortment of empty bottles lined up on the ground. The older of the two boys looked to be around twelve years old and stood a foot taller than the younger. They were both dressed in dirty jeans and faded t-shirts —splotches of the original color still evident around the neckline and sleeves.

"No like this…"

The older boy, who resembled a rabbit, with round, brown eyes and large front teeth, instructed the younger how to throw with a sharp flick of the wrist. The younger boy, who sported a nest of tight black curls, tried again.

Dust spit up around the bottles after each rock missed its target. The older boy brutally twisted the younger's ear and smacked the back of his head. Rami winced and turned his attention back to Marwan. "Do those boys have names?" He asked.

Marwan looked out into the street. "The big one is Rafik. The small one… Yasser. They both live nearby."

"I know that the old school has closed but is there no other school?"

"School?" An edge of bitterness colored Marwan's tone. He set a soda bottle on the table and popped the cap off. *Fizzzt.* "Anyone who can get a teaching job ends up leaving —like you did. They've gone to Jordan, Lebanon, Qatar, wherever there is work." He smiled scornfully as he slid the bottle to his brother.

Rami took a sip of the cola. The bubbles splashed around in his mouth and tickled the back of his throat as he swallowed. He placed the bottle carefully down —his hand wet from the sweating glass—and looked out absently at the rippling waves of heat in the distance. The day was going to be a scorcher, no question. He sensed that the suffocating climate was only a hint of troubling times to come. His stomach twisted leaving no room for any kind of an appetite. He turned back to Marwan and stared into his eyes.

"Did you know?" he asked.

A few miles away, Major Shani sat silently at his desk in his home with a wicker-framed photo positioned in front of him. He and Moshe were barely ten years old when the photo was taken. They were both wearing soccer shirts, with Moshe's arm wrapped around his best friend's shoulder —an impish grin on his chubby face that stole the spotlight from the trophy in Shani's hand. Those early years on the settlement were filled with long days of kicking the ball around until both their mothers had to physically drag them back home for dinner. They would have fun betting on whose mother would be out there first. Moshe always won.

The settlements back then were nothing more than quickly constructed camps surrounded by wire fences and guards. Small soccer tournaments organized by a few adults had helped to keep the younger children busy, offering friendships and a sense of solidarity along the way. Moshe and Shani had become inseparable — playful rivals when practicing —an unstoppable duo when competing against others.

Shani smiled sadly and looked out the window. The reflection from the water in the small wading pool danced against the garden wall. Beyond this, he could hear the rhythmic batting of a ball coming from the direction of the settlement's tennis courts. How much had changed since he was a boy?

He rolled a cigarette between two fingers and flicked open the lighter. He imagined Moshe standing in front of the bookstore on that fateful day —the same charismatic smile from the photo plastered across his face as he teased Shani over the phone. His hands would have been loaded with books, which he loved to read and loved to share information from even more. He always started a conversation with *'I read in a book…'* and this made Shani smile again. How many times had he heard him say that? His eyes welled up as he recalled his friend's body —the smell of charred flesh, hair, and blood. He leaned back in his chair and took a long hard drag from his cigarette, watching the smoke as it curled upward and filled the room. Moshe was gone. Shani would never hear his warm, spirited voice again. His grief hung in the air as thick as the smoke.

"Hey!"

Startled back to the present, Shani's eyes darted across the room.

"Don't smoke around the girls!"

Shani quickly relaxed when he saw his wife standing in the doorway. Dalya's arms were crossed, her hazel eyes resolute, but her warm smile instantly melted away all of the tension in his body.

"Sorry," he rasped, his voice hoarse. He took the cigarette from between his lips, crushed off the ember, and tucked the butt away into his shirt pocket.

Dalya walked gracefully towards him. "Thank you." She found her way into his lap. "You know I hate those things."

Shani nodded, brushed back her long raven hair, and kissed her.

"And, we don't have to go to my mother's," she continued.

'No, no, you and the girls go. I have things to do."

"But, I want to be with you. I want *us* to be with you."

"I'll be fine."

They both knew he was lying; a swarm of thoughts had buzzed around his head all night keeping him from sleep. He'd been thinking of the duties he needed to carry out during and after Hassan Amar's burial. There was sure to be an incident, and he hoped he could contain his anger and grief well enough to regain control without making things worse.

Dalya remained silent. She was well aware of her husband's apprehension. After a moment her eyes wandered to the photograph on the desk. She reached over and gently touched Moshe's image. "He was such a good friend."

"He was my best friend!" Shani realized how hard that sounded, and his voice softened. "I still can't believe he's gone. I miss him."

"I know." Taking his hand to her lips, Dalya kissed it gently. "I'll get the girls ready." She stood up about to leave when she abruptly turned back, cupped his face, and looked deeply into his eyes. "Be careful!" She stared at him for a long moment until she was sure he'd heard her.

He smiled and nodded before watching her walk out of the room. "Be careful," he repeated to himself. As a soldier, he'd spent his entire career being careful. How he looked forward to the day when he would not have to *be careful* anymore.

He'd always considered himself a pessimistic optimist —someone who believed in preparing for the worst, but who also believed that the worst would inevitably lead to growth. This was an easy philosophy to embrace in the past when horrific occurrences had not affected him directly. But, how could he possibly grow from Moshe's brutal death? And, what if one of his daughters or his wife had been standing in front of that bookstore? When he envisioned that, his rage resurfaced and images of loading his gun replayed over and over again in his head.

His thoughts turned to Moshe's funeral. He'd been able to restrain his emotions all the way there; but when he walked into the temple and saw his best friend's mother in tears, he could no longer contain himself. He hugged her as if he were tethering them both to the Earth, afraid that if he let go they would both float away on a gale of grief. They'd said nothing; only gasped for breath between inconsolable tears. When he finally drew away from her, his anger returned. He was sickened that this woman, whom he had loved since childhood, was in so much pain. He hated Dr. Amar for creating the child that had killed his best friend. He yearned for justice. His anger seemed contagious. Within moments, the anguished question *Why?* And cries for revenge from the bereaved punctuated the temple. *How quickly grief can dissolve into violence*, he thought.

Shani hated Israeli funerals, but he hated Palestinian funerals more. These were not quiet affairs. They were often incendiary enough to burst out of control. He had not supervised one since he was a newly promoted Major so many years ago and that unsettled him. He needed to be rested...

prepared. The rage of the participants was often directed at the soldiers standing by. This is why Dalya was concerned for his safety, and rightly so, but he had a job to do, and he was determined to do it to the best of his ability. He *had* to compartmentalize his emotions. He picked up the photograph, opened his desk drawer, and gently placed it inside.

Chapter 6

The early morning air was filled with the sweet chirps of a Goldfinch as Rami sat sipping tea by the kitchen window, his thoughts drifting between his family and the bird's melodious song. Minutes later, the Israeli Defense Forces were at the door. They delivered Hassan's body and then quickly and quietly retreated. As if on cue, the tiny bird flew off leaving Rami staring at his son — unable to move — with Lyda's guttural sobs barely registering.

When Rami eventually found the strength to rise, Marwan entered the house with his wife Rose, who headed straight for her sister-in-law and ushered her away. Marwan walked to his brother's side and waited silently for a while, taking in what was left of his nephew before gently bumping against Rami's shoulder.

"Let's get him ready."

Rami nodded absently and followed. The body was already sterile having been returned from the morgue, but for Rami and his brother, this was the ritual necessary before burial.

The kitchen table was the best place to lay Hassan down. As they prepared the warm water and cloth to clean him, all of Rami's medical experience departed. He felt light-headed and braced himself on the back of a chair, certain he was about to faint. Marwan noticed and kept a steady eye on his brother as he dipped the white cloth into the clay bowl and wrung it out. When Rami had regained at least some equilibrium, he made his way back to the table, clearing away the chairs by pushing them against the wall. Still, his legs felt like pails of wet cement —his whole body wanting to sink into the earth where his son would soon be buried.

Marwan handed him the warm cloth, and, without looking, Rami took it, his eyes fixed on the lacerations torn erratically across Hassan's chest. Metal and glass from the blast had ripped its way across the soft tissue. Rami's heart dropped at the thought of his son feeling such a thing, and he found himself lightly tracing the gashes with the cloth as if somehow soothing the wounds. He needed to feel the pain his son had felt before he died. He needed to punish himself — to blame himself for Hassan's unconscionable act. Guilt had clung to him ever since the phone call in Bucharest. Somehow he had known Hassan was the bomber. His rib cage felt heavy; the knot in his stomach seemed to move around, unable to settle in one place.

Rami put his hand on his son's cold skin and then cleaned the rest of the body with the same soft, soothing strokes. He was aware that if his son had been wearing a suicide vest there would be little left to clean. Hassan's injuries wrapped around his chest and back, but his legs, though heavily bruised, were still intact. Rami filed this detail away as quickly as it had registered. He could not think about that now —not now as he gently wiped his boy's brow and bathed his ashen skin.

Every so often he looked up to see Lyda wander by the kitchen like a ghost. Her face, still swollen around the eyes, could not disguise the elegant beauty that sang to his heart so many years ago. After a while, he heard her retreat to the main room where she waited with Rose, her helplessness evident in her soft whimpering.

When Hassan was eventually wrapped in white linen and brought out to the main room, the closest male relatives were the first to arrive and gather around the body. Soon after, others followed until the house slowly filled with grieving sobs and labored breath. As prayers were recited from the Koran, Rami's mind wandered outside to the sun and fresh air, which he so desperately craved.

The funeral procession drifted slowly from the house down the winding dirt lane and into the town. Rami watched Lyda and Marwan disappear, as the crowd grew larger. He wanted to be with his wife —to walk beside her and whisper words of comfort into her ear, but the distance between them was too great.

The crowd gained momentum, moving like a swift current through the streets, as young men yelled and chanted from the Koran — placards of Hassan dancing up and down about them. The coffin, draped in the Palestinian flag, floated above everyone's head on a sea of hands —the lightness of the sixteen-year-old body inside weighing heavily on Rami's aching heart. He could bear it no longer and stood off to the side watching as if he were on the banks of a raging river, unable to cross. The masses blurred into a surreal carousel of color and motion, hypnotizing him into a sickening stupor. He rocked back and forth overwhelmed by the frenetic energy saturating the air —praying that more violence would not erupt because of his son.

Keeping their distance, Israeli troops surrounded the town prepared for aggression. Rami resented their presence but understood that they needed to ensure the coffin and crowd made their way to the cemetery without incident. At funerals such as this, there were often threats of retaliation —angry youth thirsty for blood adopting violence as the path to manhood. Many of the soldiers were the same age as the young men in the crowd, adding to the tension. He looked at their faces, which were nervous but alert. They were keenly aware that this was the worst part of their job.

Shani sat in his jeep, which was parked behind Corporal Cohen and a small group of soldiers, as the rowdy multitude passed. He instinctively pulled his sidearm out and checked to see that it was loaded. As he holstered his gun, he saw Marwan take Rami's arm and guide him protectively through the crowd towards his wife, causing his own loss to wash over him once again.

As more brazen young men joined the procession, the throng became louder and angrier. A stone suddenly jettisoned toward the soldiers, followed by a volley of rocks. The soldiers shielded themselves from the impact.

"Don't shoot unless you see a gun," Cohen instructed.

"So, don't kill them unless they kill us first?" mumbled a young private who was far too green for Shani's taste. Shani could hear the fear in the soldier's voice. He looked over as more rocks flew towards the soldiers, one bouncing off the private's helmet. Before Corporal Cohen could stop him, the young man had raised his M16 and squeezed off several rounds of rubber bullets, which flew dangerously close to the crowd. Terrified, the crowd ducked for cover as the other soldiers raised their weapons.

"Stand down!" Cohen shouted, fearing that a riot might ensue. When the soldiers reluctantly lowered their weapons, all that could be heard were the whimpers of frightened women and children over the echo of the shots still ringing in the valley.

Rami stood up and glared at Cohen who looked back at him apologetically and then nodded, indicating that it was safe to proceed. The crowd slowly reassembled, cautiously continuing down the road, but

Rami's attention shifted to Shani who was standing in his jeep gritting his teeth in fury. Shani knew that this incident would further erode the doctor's trust in him, and this was not what he wanted. He needed Dr. Amar to be forthcoming during the investigation. He turned away and glared into the back of the private's head willing him to feel the heat of his rage. Green or not, the soldier would soon be severely disciplined for his actions. For now, Shani signaled to Cohen who nodded and pulled the young soldier out of the ranks. The rest of the troop moved down the road maintaining a healthy distance so the mourners could reach the burial site without further incident.

Shani drove to the cemetery and swung his jeep around to face the crowd when it arrived. Still seething, he pulled a cigarette out of his pocket, lit it, and inhaled deeply feeling the calming smoke fill his lungs —no wife or daughters to give him grief. He eyed the soldiers in the vicinity. They were all more seasoned than the young private, and this helped quiet him further. The funeral would be over soon, and he could get back to his investigation.

As the crowd moved closer to Hassan's final resting place, the masses once again became braver — more defiant —but no more rocks were thrown. Rami was now beside Lyda and Marwan. He watched as Lyda put her arm through Marwan's arm for support, and felt a surge of jealousy as she rested her head against her brother-in-law's chest. He knew his brother had taken good care of her while he was gone, but now he was here and that was *his* role. Still, he had to find a way to break the wall he and Lyda had built around themselves —a goal that seemed a thousand years away. He pushed his jealousy back down reminding himself to be grateful for those he once took for granted. Marwan and Lyda were all he had left.

When they arrived at the cemetery, Rami noticed the Major and stopped. The two men stood staring at one another —the coffin floating between them on restless hands. It caught Shani's attention making him feel nauseated. He coughed and spit into the dirt. Again, he was angry. Again, he hated everyone and everything. But, regaining his focus, he nodded to Rami to assure him that his troops were under control.

When the coffin was finally laid down, the crowd gathered and the Imam began reciting from the scriptures. His words of solace counterpointed Lyda's unbridled sobs. Hesitating at first, Rami moved toward his wife and put his arm around her, but it did little to arrest her tears. He could feel her body tremble —her breath trapped in her lungs, buckling and shivering. The full gravity of their world pressed down on them as if they were being sucked into the very earth they stood on. He wanted to drop to the ground and lay there holding her, but instead, he gently took her hand — Hassan's name echoing in his mind like the haunting song of the morning goldfinch.

He stopped listening to the Imam and looked up. He could feel the wind on his face —warm, familiar, and calming. Closing his eyes, he tried to focus on hearing only the wind and what it was trying to tell him now that he was putting his son into the ground —now that it was all too real —now that his heart had shattered into a million tiny pieces. He listened and listened as the breeze picked up. But its whispers were hollow.

Chapter 7

Once again, Rami found himself waking up in his living room chair. He looked through the small window and could see morning was about to break —the sky shimmering somewhere between the artifacts of night and the uncertainty of the coming day. He had slept in his clothes again and could feel the creases digging into his skin, making him feel older than his years. His insides felt bruised and his head throbbed —the ache of exhaustion folding over his neck and shoulders. He rubbed his face to get some feeling back and tried to stand up straight, stretching slowly until the small of his back popped. He needed to begin sleeping horizontally again, he thought.

He stood there for a moment unsure of what to do until he saw his prayer mat leaning against the wall and thought about unraveling it. A sudden, fervent pounding at the door caused him to jump. Flattening his hair with his palms, he approached the door wondering who could be so rude this early in the morning. He was surprised to find Major Shani standing on the other side of the threshold with his men gathered behind him. Shani's expression was bleak and distant —his eyes cryptic.

"We need to speak."

Rami looked past the Major and silently counted the number of soldiers in his front garden. "All of us?" he asked calmly.

Moments later, the two men were sitting in the living room facing one another. Lyda could be heard rattling around in the kitchen, and judging by the slamming of cupboards, it was clear how she felt about their uninvited guest. When she finally appeared with two cups of coffee on a small tray, she calmly set it down in front of them without acknowledging either man. Shani looked to the doorway where Corporal Cohen dutifully waited. The Corporal nodded and quickly intercepted Lyda to escort her outside. She was visibly shocked when he asked her to wait in one of the vehicles where he would question her later. She obliged silently, but her expression was one of contempt.

Inside, the silence between the two men was palpable. Shani used the quietude to scan every nook and crevice of the room. Like most of the other homes in the village it was humble — small and uncluttered, and built of unassuming cinder blocks — a rectangle of gray rectangles. A few family photos decorated the walls and several cushions offered some color to the faded couch and chairs, but beyond this, the furnishings were functional and ordinary. Regardless of its simplicity, Shani was certain the house would stand for hundreds of years if not for what he was about to do.

Rami reached for his cup. Despite who was sitting in her living room, his wife would never let a guest drink a bad cup of coffee. He smiled at her pride. Sipping, he made the sound of a man enjoying a good brew, mimicking the campy commercials he'd watched on Romanian television. He wanted to remind the Major that he would not be intimidated in his own home.

Shani watched, allowing Rami to savor what would be the last cup of coffee he would have in that chair, in this house. When Rami finally put down his cup, the major's gravelly voice shattered the peace.

"Who was Hassan involved with? The Zahal Allah?"

Rami looked up dispassionately. "I know nothing. I was not around."

"So, you didn't know any of the people he was involved with?"

"No."

Shani waited to let the silence between them amplify. Then, with a hint of sympathy, he asked, "Did you two stay in touch? Were you close?"

"I encouraged him to write letters."

"I'll need to see those. Are they with you?"

Rami could not lie because they would find Hassan's letters in his suitcase. They were the first things he'd packed. He nodded as he tried to remember if there was anything incriminating in the letters — anything he'd missed. Were there any details that might be deemed significant? He could think of nothing. Although he had relished each hand-written page from his son, the letters were, for the most part, short and uneventful —evidence of Hassan's anger towards him. Rami felt certain the IDF would come to the same conclusion. He rose and retrieved the bound letters from his suitcase in the bedroom. Handing them over to the Major, he sat back down wondering if he would ever see them again. "There are only five. He was not prolific."

"I can see that," returned Shani as he perused the letters quickly. "And they appear to be fairly non-descript. Not surprising, I suppose, for a resentful fifteen-year-old."

Rami remained silent. The Major was astute, and there was an edge to his bluntness that was disquieting. Still, Shani leaned forward and handed the letters back.

"There is nothing of value here, and I would be sorry to deprive a father of his son's last letters."

Rami nodded and carefully rebound the collection of envelopes with a blue ribbon.

"Was there anything you noticed? Did he mention anything new in his life, any changes in his behavior?"

"I know nothing, I wasn't around."

"Yes, you said that already."

Rami shifted in his seat for the first time showing some discomfort in being interrogated. The fact was he didn't know what happened to his son or who had encouraged him to make the decisions he made. Yet, when he'd received the phone call in Bucharest, he knew that his son was dead —that he had done something terrible. There were no clues in Hassan's letters that indicated he'd become involved with extremists, but there was something in his voice whenever they'd spoken on the phone —a resistance — impatience —that had never been there before. Regardless, this was not something he cared to share with the IDF. He looked at the Major and shook his head.

Seeing that he was getting nowhere, Shani changed direction, trying to steer the conversation to something less accusatory. "How do you like teaching in Bucharest?"

"I am fortunate to have the work."

"And you were educated in Beirut?"

'Yes, your file is correct. And my favorite color is blue, and my favorite fruit is pomegranate. Anything else? Perhaps you'd like to know what I eat for breakfast every morning, or how many times I go to the bathroom?"

Shani had expected this to be difficult. His brow furled, and he quickly decided to devise another tactic. He reached for his coffee and lightly blew on it before he sipped. His throat felt raw and he swallowed loudly, but the liquid was pleasantly satisfying —just hot enough to feel it all the way down into his belly, making him realize his stomach was empty. He could not remember the last time he'd eaten; violence could erupt and escalate so quickly in the West Bank, putting him in a constant state of alert that made most meals rushed or non-existent. This seemed to have diminished his appetite in general. Now, Lyda's rich fragrant blend filled the emptiness in his gut. He looked up, the satisfaction evident on his face.

"This is very good."

"What? Did you think it was poisoned?"

Shani smiled. He could easily imagine the enraged and grieving Lyda slipping cyanide, or whatever awful thing she could find in the kitchen, into his coffee.

Remembering his wife, Rami turned and gazed through the open door to see Corporal Cohen in the back seat of the Jeep with her. He watched as the Corporal lifted his pen and began bombarding her with questions. Lyda stared blankly ahead as silent as stone.

Cohen finally gave up. Throwing the pad down, he reached into his pocket for a cigarette and shoved it into his mouth. As he flicked his lighter, Lyda turned and quickly snatched the cigarette from between his lips, snapped it in half, and threw it into the dirt. Rami held back a smile.

"It's such a beautiful city, Beirut," Shani continued, pulling the doctor's attention back into the living room. It's a shame Israelis cannot visit a place that's so close."

"Some have," Rami reminded him. "Occupation has its rewards."

Shani did not take this salvo personally. "Doctor, I have three daughters who mean the world to me. I am fortunate for this gift. If life is truly great, I will die before them, but until then I will do everything in my power to keep them safe. That is my job as a father."

Rami suddenly realized that he had not thought of the man in front of him as anything other than an adversary. Of course, he had a family. But why was he telling him this now? Then it dawned on him. "You have some Western training," he observed.

"What makes you say that?" Shani put down his cup.

"Your attempts to ingratiate yourself with me — to find some common ground between us so that I might let down my guard and possibly confess to something. Smells American."

Shani scrutinized Rami for a moment, and then with a laugh admitted, "A few of us did train with an FBI's anti-terrorist task force when we were in the States; but they learned more from us."

Rami rose abruptly no longer in the mood for the Major's interrogation tactics. "If that is all, I need to pray." He had no intention of praying; he was using his own tactics in the hope the Major would respect his needs and leave.

Shani remained seated clearly indicating who was in charge. "Dr. Amar, I've spoken to others. I now know why you left Beit Jbal. It took courage to do what you did." He was surprised at his own words and let this revelation sink in as Rami slowly sat back down in his chair. "Regardless, I must hold your travel documents. You are not permitted to leave."

"But my work? My students? How long will you keep me prisoner?"

Shani's expression hardened. "For as long as it takes to complete the investigation." He looked around the house —the family photos; the furniture that had seen better days; and the prayer rug rolled up and leaning against the wall. He didn't agree with what he was about to do —*collective punishment* as a deterrent against terrorism made no sense to him. Why punish family members who were already grief-stricken when all it appeared to achieve was more pain and hostility? But orders were orders. Standing, he could not hide the regret in his eyes. Rami gripped the arm of his chair; he could see that the Major was struggling with whatever he was about to say.

"We must search your home again. Afterwards, you will have thirty minutes to gather your things before we raze it."

Rami sat dumfounded; the word "raze" ringing in his ears. He knew this might happen, but not so quickly, and certainly not now. His heart sank at the thought of his house being leveled right in front of him. He swallowed hard, everything suddenly feeling surreal.

"You're actually going through with it?" He felt betrayed and wondered why. Neither Shani nor the IDF owed him anything. His son had killed their citizens. What did he expect? This was just the beginning. He and Lyda could be thrown in jail indefinitely if they felt they had cause. Rami shook his head. "*Thirty minutes to gather your things*," he repeated. "As if a lifetime of living could be gathered up in thirty minutes."

"I sympathize, but these are my orders." Shani walked to the door. "I'm sorry," he added. He nodded to Corporal Cohen, who exited the jeep and strode swiftly to his side. "Make it quick," Shani said flatly before exiting. Cohen turned and ordered his soldiers inside.

When the soldiers had completed their task, Rami returned Hassan's letters to his suitcase, and then quickly enlisted his neighbors to help empty the house. Marwan and Rose arrived and organized everyone into small groups, each responsible for a different room. Rami was deciding what he and Lyda needed the most, and what could be sacrificed, when he heard his distraught wife in the front garden. He hurried out to find her screaming at the soldiers who stood guard. They did their best to ignore her but she was shrill and hysterical.

"Do your mothers know what you're doing to people's homes —to their families? This is insane! We had nothing to do with the bombing! Nothing!" She turned her rage on Shani, who was sitting in his jeep watching quietly. "How could you do this? We've done nothing wrong!"

"Stop it!" Rami shouted.

Lyda swung around and glared at him; her stare as sharp as a saber. "Aren't you going to *do* something?"

"What am I supposed to do?"

"Nothing! Do *nothing* like you always do!" She turned back to the soldiers. "We've already lost our son! What more do you want from us? You're sons of whores! All of you!"

Rami grabbed her arm and pulled her close. "Stop Lyda! Go inside and help!" His jaw was clenched as his fingers dug into her flesh.

Lyda's eyes glistened. She slapped his hand away but he knew she would not provoke him further. Up until now he had been tolerant of her reactions —made room for her pain —but he was reaching his breaking point. A deep guttural noise forced its way up through her throat as she spun around and dashed inside their home. Rami stared after her for a few seconds, his body as tight as his fists. He wondered at his own capacity for violence; the coil inside him was tightly wound now and he feared it could snap any moment. He spat into the dry, caked earth, and then followed her in.

Shani puffed on his cigarette and watched the smoke disappear. While witnessing their exchange his body had tightened; he could only feel responsible for it all. Lyda was a fighter and he admired that in her. She reminded him of his own wife, adding to his remorse. He inhaled the last puff and then flicked his cigarette butt into the dirt. Checking his watch, he nodded to his underling. Corporal Cohen blew a whistle and a bulldozer engine growled to life.

At the sound, the neighbors rushed out with Rami and Lyda's belongings followed by the distraught couple. The bulldozer lunged forward and rumbled across the ground like a movable earthquake. It rammed into the front wall of the house so forcefully that everyone jumped back, shocked by the sudden impact. Dust and debris spiraled into the air. Some of the women began to cry, but the angry machine drowned out their desperate wails. Only their tortured expressions indicated the pain they felt as they watched the destruction of yet another family home.

Rami collapsed onto his couch, placed haphazardly in the street, and watched everything crumble. Lyda's voice was hoarse. She was still screaming and crying, but now in the face of Corporal Cohen who callously motioned for her to back off. Rose hurried over and quickly led her away into the arms of the other women.

As Rami took in the slow destruction of the home where they had raised Hassan, he slipped into another place, another time. The drone of the bulldozer reminded him of when they'd first built the house. It sounded like the machine they had used to level their land before laying the cinder blocks. Hassan was four years old at the time; lifting one of the blocks to bring to his *baba* was a monumental task. Still, the delight on Hassan's face was so pleasurable that Rami had cheered him on, telling him which ones to pick —not the cracked ones, or the ones already broken —good, solid concrete blocks. They were perfect every time.

Rami's head swirled with images of Hassan to the point where he no longer heard the noise of the bulldozer, the rants of his wife, nor the cries of disbelief from the neighbors shocked at the cruelty of obliterating a home for no logical reason. He felt nothing; not even the tears that streamed down his dusty face and splattered onto his clothing like rain from the heavens.

One by one the walls crumbled as the bulldozer's heavy tracks rolled relentlessly back and forth, crushing everything in their wake. When it was finally over most of the onlookers turned away, hands held to mouths, heartsick for their friends.

Gradually, Rami came to and scanned the area around him. He saw everything with such clarity now: the dirt taking shape in the air; Shani's cigarette smoke billowing up and dancing away; the soldiers standing by — unsympathetic and alert; and Lyda. She stood there looking exhausted and ready to fall. She was close enough that he could touch the back of her hand with his, and as he did, she grasped it tightly. He slowly led her backward until she came to the edge of the couch and sat down beside him. They were stunned, spent. Rami gently folded his arms around her and she leaned into him. He held her there until the sun began to set, the soldiers cleared out, and the neighbors wandered back to their lives.

Once evening crept in, all anyone could see of the couple was their silhouette still sitting on the couch — their house gone. Jagged chunks of concrete and bent nests of metal poked up through the pile of rubble like struggling plants reaching for light and air.

When Lyda pulled away and stood up, Rami watched her silently as she wandered around the ruins of their home like a ghost in a graveyard. *What does a man do now that does not betray his frailty?* He wondered.

Eventually, Marwan and Rose came forward. Rose helped Lyda extricate herself from the ruins and spirited her away to their home where food and a bed awaited.

Leaning down, Marwan placed his large hands beneath his brother's elbows and eased him up off his perch. "Come my brother...come with us."

Rami allowed Marwan to lead him away —their figures gradually disappearing into the shadows of the evening, leaving the couch empty and neglected in the stillness of the moonlit night.

Major Shani stepped out of the jeep and surveyed his home. He knew his girls were already in bed but he would head upstairs and tuck them in anyway. Coming home to his family was his favorite part of the evening — of every evening— and he never took it for granted. It was a life he would always fiercely protect — the life of a man and a woman still in love, whose children laughed and played with abandon while their parents watched over them.

Dalya was busy in the kitchen warming up his dinner when he entered. He watched as she moved gracefully toward him drying her hands on her apron.

"Hi, sweetheart. How was your day?" Kissing him, she quickly took his satchel and set it down on the nearby bench as she always did. Then, she frowned. "What's wrong?"

His wife's ability to assess his mood always amazed him. Shani couldn't hide anything from her; she knew every nuanced expression, however slight. "We destroyed his house today," he muttered, his eyes meeting hers.

His voice lingered as they walked into the cool air of the living room. He was well aware that Dalya stood firmly on the other side of the collective punishment issue. They had debated it many times over dinner and during social gatherings. The act was necessary according to her, but he was not convinced. He had witnessed the devastation firsthand. She had not. And, in Hassan Amar's case, he was now certain that the doctor and his wife were not involved. There were enough people who knew why Dr. Amar had left Beit Jbal so abruptly; that information was easy enough to find out, even for an Israeli.

"The girls are asleep?" he asked looking up at the ceiling.

"Yes, they missed you. They're waiting for you to say goodnight." Dalya put a hand on his back and guided him towards the stairs.

Shani stopped. Pulling her warm body to his, he kissed her tenderly, breathing her in.

"I'm sorry," she said when their bodies parted. " I know how you hate destroying a family's home."

"What's done is done," he replied. "But this will be the last time for me." He'd made up his mind. He would no longer participate in further traumatizing the traumatized.

Dalya nodded, choosing to remain silent. Taking her husband's hand, she led him upstairs where their girls waited patiently.

Shani just needed to see his girls in order to feel at ease… complete. Just peeking through the door to find their faces peaceful and still in the soft glow of the night-light, settled him. Sometimes he felt compelled to straighten a wrinkle or two in their blankets —perhaps a metaphor for their growing pains to come. Often, he needed to gently brush their cheeks, to feel their warmth, their innocence, which would further infuse his spirit with hope and reassurance about the job he had to do —the safer future he wished for them.

As he approached the door of their middle child, he found that Sally was still awake reading under a small light. She looked up as the door opened and the hall light spilled into the room. She smiled and put her book down, sliding lower into the bed. Shani quietly approached as was his ritual, tucked her in, and kissed her on the forehead.

'Goodnight, sweetheart!"

"Goodnight, Papa."

Chapter 8

Rami's feet felt heavy in a drag-and-drop cadence along the dusty road. White clouds kicked up and hovered around his ankles leaving a ghostly film on the hem of his trousers. He stopped, unsure of where he was or where he was going. Retrieving a handkerchief from his pocket, he snapped it out and gathered it again in one palm lifting it to the thick beads of sweat that formed on his brow. His tolerance had been reached, broken... the heat was just too much.

"The heat is too much!" Rami-startled awake. He looked around disoriented and realized that he had fallen asleep in his clothes yet again. The air was stagnant as if held in place by the sweltering temperature. He peeled off his stained shirt and sat up on the bed in his undershirt, which was just as riddled with dust and sweat. His shoes and socks had been removed and were placed neatly beside a small, ornate wooden chair. He knew the chair well —it had belonged to his mother. This was his brother's home.

He felt Lyda's stillness under the sheets and maneuvered slowly and quietly to the edge of the bed so he wouldn't disturb her. He could hear her soft breath rise and fall in a gentle rhythm and realized how much he had missed that sound while away in Bucharest.

He looked at their belongings piled against the far wall. Most of Hassan's things had been confiscated, so there were few items of emotional value in the clutter. His house was the only object he truly wanted and needed, and now it was gone. He took a deep breath and stifled the urge to cry. The pain was there but the well was dry.

As the events of the previous day slowly awakened his senses, he resigned himself to the fact that he was living in a nightmare. He studied the room and realized that he had never been in it before. The room belonged to Imad, Marwan's son, but was no longer used as Imad had disappeared some time ago. There was a photo of him with his parents on the dresser. His eyes were laughing and his smile genuine —a cigarette alive in his blurred hand. It was a relaxed moment captured in black and white.

Rami remembered how intelligent and charismatic Imad had always been, even as a boy. Everyone who crossed his path became enamored with him, and it became quickly apparent that Imad never failed to use that to his advantage.

By the age of twenty-two, Imad had become involved with the wrong people, using his charisma to accomplish much in terms of what the disillusioned and less scrupulous viewed as victories against the IDF. The Israelis had photos of him and considered him dangerous. Marwan had once said that a man with a thick black Moustache came to their doorstep one night to warn Imad that the IDF were on their way to interrogate him. Until that point, Marwan and Rose had tried to steer their son away from his nefarious dealings; but when the moustached man told Imad that the IDF would imprison him for life or, more likely, just shoot him in cold blood, they encouraged Imad to run.

To their disappointment, by thirty-two Imad was behind many of the recruits who caused the

notorious football explosion and other atrocities.
That he had been able to elude the Israeli authorities
was nothing short of miraculous. In a place with few
places to hide, he had earned the nickname *Ghost* for
his ability to be just that. This, and the loyalty he had
accumulated from the people who supported him,
made him something of a legend to both the cynical
and impressionable alike. Without this level of
backing, surely he would have been brought to
justice, or killed on sight long ago.

For this reason, a meeting with Imad was
virtually impossible, though Rami knew that he
would have to eventually press Marwan to set one
up. A flurry of questions infested his thoughts. *Did
Imad know? Was he aware of who encouraged
Hassan? Did he have anything to do with Hassan's
actions?* It seemed in all likelihood that he did. It was
all too unsettling. Rami closed his eyes thinking
again of Hassan. His room was gone forever —no
more listening to music on his bed, reading the
books on his small bookshelf, or calling his parents
in to say goodnight

While in Romania, guilt haunted him when he
thought of his family and friends back home. But he
knew that he could not return. He could not do what the

angry and violent had asked of him. These were not the things his doctor hands were trained to do. These were not the things anyone should do. To provide healing was bliss. To destroy another human was simply not in his DNA. He'd had no choice he told himself. He had to flee or they would force the worst upon him.

As he attempted to rise from the bed, the weight of his emotions fell on him again, and he sank back into the mattress grasping his chest. The moment of panic quickly subsided as he remembered the heart attack-like symptoms associated with anxiety. He put his fingers to his pulse and took several deep breaths. When he was ready, he rose again, slowly this time, determined to push forward and see the day through.

Outside, the morning air was already soup-like and the sun's dazzling light unyielding. Rami's eyes struggled to focus. He had borrowed a clean shirt from Marwan's closet and was thankful for its thinness and over-large size. Still, his underarms were already soaked, and his feet felt like two cement bricks.

When he stopped to wipe his brow with his handkerchief, he saw Marwan's café —its rippled green awning and cheap plastic furniture now a welcomed sight. He put the handkerchief away and continued forward as his brother stepped out into the sunlight.

Always the accommodating host, Marwan received his brother with open arms. "Rami, my brother! May I tempt you once again with one of my famous French omelets?" He pulled out one of the light plastic chairs and motioned for Rami to sit.

"Just water," Rami replied, as he sat and wiped his brow again. "Too early to be this hot!"

"That it is, brother! That it is! But let me make you something. You *must* eat something, even if you don't feel hungry right now." Marwan came around with a cold bottle of water.

Rami tipped the icy water back and wondered what would happen next. What would he do? He had no home and he could not return to work. How long was he expected to stay at his brother's house? For that matter, the IDF may come tomorrow and destroy that house too. After all, Marwan was family and must be a suspect also.

Rami looked at his brother and wondered again if he should suspect Marwan of not telling him all that he knew. He watched his brother turn and busy himself behind the counter. There were so many questions he *needed* to ask him, but perhaps now was not the time.

As he tipped the cold bottle back again, his eyes landed on Rafik and Yasser playing in the middle of the street.

"Aim like you're hitting a bird," instructed Rafik

"Ouch!" Yasser's face contorted in pain as he took another knock on the head from his friend.

Rami hated that they weren't in school. "Those boys should have the guidance of a teacher and not be acting like delinquents! Call them over, Marwan!"

Marwan shouted to them and the boys stopped, begrudgingly dragging their feet into the café, until he handed each of them a drink.

Marwan returned to his post behind the counter, while Rafik and Yasser stood sheepishly next to Rami with the colas in their hands.

"The school may be closed but why aren't you learning somewhere else?" Rami asked.

"We are," Rafik replied with a frown. He was a coarse-haired boy with eyes that seemed to have the depth of a quarry. Rami thought his puckered frown was much too adult for his years. The child had boyhood features but his attitude and gestures were that of an angry adult —gestures he'd undoubtedly picked up from a strong, male family member.

Rami studied them both feeling he understood their souls. These young boys were typical of what had happened to many of the boys in the region. They were deeply influenced by rage and mistrust. "You are in school? Now?"

"Yes, the street is our school. We are practicing our aim, so we can kill Jews."

Rami leaned back in his chair. The boy was too matter-of-fact about the taking of life. He took a moment and then continued carefully. "So this is your plan? To kill *people* with stones?"

"Jews," repeated Rafik.

"*People*," returned Rami. "*Jews* are people like you and me."

They both looked at him quizzically, not sure of his tone as they quietly sipped their drinks.

Rami looked over to Marwan who busied himself wiping imaginary stains on the countertop.

"Besides, the real school has been closed forever and it's a mess," piped up Yasser. "It was practically destroyed from the shelling last year."

Turning to him, Rami was reminded again that these boys, like all the children in this place, had been forced to grow up too quickly. The unstable environment would not let them be little boys; they had to be little men. It was evident in their words and actions: how they waved their arms when they spoke; the way they clasped their hands behind their backs as they walked; the bearing in their stride; even in the manner in which they finished their drinks with a satisfying gasp of air and a hearty slam of the bottles on the table. These were all traits of bravado adopted consciously or otherwise from their fathers, uncles, and older brothers.

"Marwan, two more colas for these young men!" Rami ordered, to the wide-eyed delight of the boys.

"The little fart is right! There is barely anything left." Rafik concurred. "The school is full of bullet holes, and then a boulder rolled down the hill and hit one of the walls."

Marwan set two more bottles down on the table. The boys eyed them with anticipation as the condensation glistened off the glass. Neither reached for them. Rami understood their hesitation and handed them each one. They immediately brought the bottles to their lips. Rami leaned forward. "Tell me about the boul…"

"Mount Yasser we call it," interrupted Yasser.

"Mount Arafat," corrected Rafik, as he punched Yasser in the arm.

Yasser rolled his eyes. Naming the boulder was a constant dispute between them. "And now it sits in the middle of the playing field," he added, sticking his tongue out at Rafik.

"I see," said Rami.

"Not only is the school destroyed, but we can't even have a game of football on the field."

Rami was silent for a moment and then said, "I should go see for myself."

They looked at him curiously, shrugged their shoulders, and finished their drinks with a long, satisfying belch followed immediately by uncontrollable, giddy laughter.

Rami smiled sadly. In some things, they would always be little boys.

Chapter 9

Major Shani sat in his small study reviewing surveillance documents and photos of Rami. The photos were recent —Rami outside the guard post, walking in the street and sitting at his brother's café. Shani took a moment and sat back in his chair, uncertain of what he was looking for. He could hear his wife and daughters in the kitchen preparing lunch.

As he returned to the photos, one in particular caught his attention. He was so transfixed with its contents that he didn't notice his wife entering the room. The photo was of Rami sitting in the café speaking to two young boys. Judging by their body language, it appeared they would rather be anywhere else. Then Shani's gaze wandered over to the picture of him and Moshe as boys, which he had returned to his desk in a moment of weakness. His mind began to drift. When Dalya gently placed her hand on his shoulder, he jumped.

"Oh, sorry. You're so tense. Lunch is ready. Come and eat with us," she coaxed.

"I'm not hungry, darling."

"You should eat something, sweetheart. Cigarettes kill your appetite. If you don't eat you will get sick. Nobody wants that. Besides, the girls want to show you what polite ladies they can be.."

He paused. The photo was buckling beneath his hot hands. He was already too consumed with the case. He quickly scooped up the rest of the file, tossed it into his drawer, and slammed it shut. "Yes, sure. How could I miss that?"

As they entered the kitchen, the girls were already serving lunch. Lissette, the oldest at twelve, put the last plate on the table as Sally helped their youngest sister, Hofit, onto her usual chair.

It was a veritable feast. At the table's center there was a wooden bowl filled with lettuce, fresh tomatoes, and cucumbers from the garden, and sprinkled with lemon juice, olive oil, and tangy sumac spice. The hummus plate had a rustic, gritty texture under the olive oil, which glistened in a pool at its center; and the skewers of chicken spiced with sweet paprika, lemon, and cumin, had been grilled over charcoal and drizzled with the same, ever-present, oil.

Shani smiled at his daughters as he and Dalya found their seats. "What a nice looking lunch!"

Hofit awkwardly attempted to scoop salad onto her plate. Everyone watched her struggle but knew her stubbornness would not allow any assistance. Finally, Shani teased, "Can I help you with that?"

"Nope, I got it!"

She was one of the most confident five-year-olds he had ever known, and he looked at his wife and winked, proud of their little one's fierce independence.

"The proper response is, *No thank you*," Sally corrected. Being the middle child, she liked to distinguish herself as Hofit's superior.

"No thank you, papa," Hofit repeated.

"If you're done, maybe we can have some too!" Lissette was getting impatient. Hofit paid no attention. She made one last attempt and managed to grab three tomatoes and a lettuce leaf. Everyone laughed, including Hofit, as only the lettuce leaf found her plate.

As Shani watched his girls fill their plates, his thoughts drifted back to the last photo he was studying — Rami with the two young boys. *Who were they? What were they discussing?* These were not "sit-at-the- dinner-table" boys. These were boys who wandered. These were the exact type of boys that worried Shani. They were the kind that could grow up in the wrong direction —could grow up to hurt others —hurt his girls. Hofit crunched down on her lettuce leaf. *He was never going to let that happen.*

Chapter 10

Rami walked along the dusty road kicking up pebbles now and then until he reached a stone staircase on the hillside. He slowly climbed the debris-covered steps —his knees feeling increasingly sore as he ascended. The tall, unkempt grass edged the arc of the staircase, acting as an imaginary railing, guiding him on.

The building ahead had been abandoned for some time. The walls were barely visible above the tall grass and were badly damaged by stray mortar shells and bullets. Rami realized that it would require a lot more than a few bricks and a coat of paint to restore his former school. He reached into his pocket, snapped open his handkerchief, and dabbed the moisture from his brow.

Turning his attention to the adjacent playing field, he saw the boulder —Mount Yasser or Mount Arafat —sitting undisturbed and as large as a small mountain at its center. The boulder's shadow stretched to the broken stone wall that now intermittently surrounded the schoolyard. As he traced its path, he could see that the rock had rolled down from an adjacent hill behind the school, clipping the corner wall and tearing the bricks apart before it came to rest.

He stepped past the jagged bricks and entered what was left of the building to survey the ruined interior. A few chairs and desks lay on their sides amid broken glass and splintered wood. Rami pursed his lips and shook his head. None of this was fair or right.

As he made his way to the spot where Miss Malouf once sat, he spotted something beneath an overturned chair. Squatting down he pulled out an old, frayed textbook —the spine dangling on long, silvery threads. He could hear his favorite teacher's voice echoing across the dusty room and whispering in his ear. Then... a bold idea began to take form.

He made his way back out over the fragmented steps that once brought young students into this room and filled their minds with knowledge. Scanning the landscape beyond, he breathed in slowly and deeply. *Where there is life, there's hope*, he thought, and his lips gradually parted into a smile.

Inside the guard station, Shani had set up a temporary workspace to study the files on Rami when Corporal Cohen knocked and entered.

"Dr. Amar is here to see you, sir."

"Here? To see me?" Shani was perplexed.

"Yes, sir."

"Send him in…uh did you search him?"

"Of course, " proclaimed Cohen as he turned to leave.

"*Yes or no* is all I need, Corporal!" Shani was annoyed. He was not fond of Cohen, whom he found pitiless and far too riddled with self-importance.

Cohen turned to face him, remembering his station. "Sorry sir. Yes, Major, sir!" He quickly exited to retrieve the Doctor.

Shani slid the documents into a drawer and placed his family photo face down as Rami entered. The Doctor was wiping his brow with his handkerchief, but he looked surprisingly invigorated.

"Doctor Amar, what brings you here today? Do you have some new bit of information that will help our investigation?"

"Nothing of the sort. I have come to ask for your help."

"*My* help? I don't understand." Now Shani was even more confused.

"May I?" Indicating the chair across from Shani, Rami waited for a nod before sitting. "I need bricks, cement, paint, a blackboard, chalk, pencils, paper... I have a complete list here." He pulled a neatly folded piece of paper from his shirt pocket and handed it over.

Shani felt as if he'd entered the conversation midway through. He scanned the paper quickly and then dropped it on the desk. "I don't understand. What does this have to do with me?"

"This has everything to do with you. You will not let me leave, so I must make use of myself while I am here."

There was an air of determination in the doctor that Shani had not witnessed before. Still, his request was entirely incongruous. "What you do with your time here is no concern of mine… unless you're plotting to kill my countrymen."

"There are boys in the street who should be in school and yet all they are doing is learning to hate you and your countrymen."

That explains the photo, thought Shani. "What else is new?"

Rami took a deep breath and calmed himself; he was too excited and it showed. If he was going to get through to the Major, he needed to slow down and apply the strategies he'd learned as a physician when dealing with distressed families. He met the Major's eyes composed and sincere.

"These things I ask for are easy for you to acquire from the nearest settlement, even your settlement. Here we have nothing, as you well know. We can do so much with so little, but we do need at least a little."

Shani looked at Rami, impressed by his resolve. This man was not going to give up. "And if I do these things for you, what do I get in return? What will you do for me?"

"I will teach them not to kill you…or your men… or your family."

"You certainly set high goals for yourself." The Major leaned forward and grabbed his cigarette pack from beside the desk lamp.

"And I will offer you some free medical advice."

Shani's eyebrows raised.

"Stop smoking and see a throat specialist."

Shani put the cigarettes back down. "What makes you think…"

"You're a chain smoker. Your voice is hoarse. You have difficulty swallowing, and you've lost weight since we first met. My guess is your appetite has diminished as well."

Shani sat back in his chair, eyeing Rami curiously. Rami could see his reaction was neither defensive nor indignant.

Picking up the list on his desk, the Major was silent for a moment. "Let me give this some thought," he said finally.

"That is all I ask."

"Well, if that is all, I have work to do."

Rami took the cue and began to leave, but as he reached the door he stopped and turned. "And since I no longer have a home, the items can be delivered to my brother's café. I presume you know where that is." He turned back, opened the door, and disappeared into the bleach-bright sunlight.

Shani looked at the empty doorway, a sudden feeling of foreboding weighing him down. When was the last time he'd been to his doctor? He couldn't remember. What did Dr. Amar suspect? This was the perfect moment to light up a cigarette and think, but the package remained untouched.

He opened the doctor's list again and attempted to focus on his requests. Shani's thinking was usually methodical, but now his thoughts wandered looking for a place to settle.

Putting his hands to his neck, he swallowed back his saliva. His gulp was loud and his throat raw. For months now he'd felt like he was on the verge of a cold, but a virus never seemed to manifest. What other symptoms had he ignored? He pressed his fingers into the tender flesh beneath his jaw and ran them towards his earlobes. Swollen glands. His gravelly voice... his weight loss... he had shrugged everything off as the result of stress and lack of sleep. Now Rami Amar —this man he had hated — was suggesting it was something more. Picking up his phone, he dialed his doctor's number.

Once his appointment was made, Shani tried to focus on the list again. School supplies. The doctor wanted to teach the youth in the area right from wrong. He wanted to steer them away from vengeance towards reason. The first step that Shani needed to take, if he was going to help him, was to fully accept that Dr. Amar was not his enemy. But, if he wasn't his enemy, then what was he? Shani refolded the list, stood up, and looked through the tiny window.

The doctor had become a specter in the distance, the chalky dust from the roadside obscuring his feet. His otherworldly form looked lonely against the parched landscape. Shani realized he had a begrudging admiration for the man. He was impressed by his steely determination and bold requests. He had managed to attain a good education and a noble, honorable profession amidst adversity. He appeared to be a principled man who had dedicated his life to helping and healing others. By his nature alone, he could help better the small part of the world in which they lived.

Shani also conceded that the doctor's audacity seemed to imply they shared a history. In a sense, they did —collectively as a people at least — so there was that. But, unbeknownst to the doctor, they also had grief in common — both having lost someone they loved dearly in the same pointless tragedy. The doctor's striving to make a difference was an atonement of sorts —a baby step toward peace. Bold initiatives had come and gone in this volatile region, but they were often one-sided.

Perhaps joining forces would yield better, longer-lasting results. Still, Shani was uncertain.

"Baby steps," he mumbled.

Chapter 11

As Rami walked back to Marwan's house, he mulled over his encounter with the Major. He believed their conversation had gone well, and was proud of the way he had handled things so calmly and decisively. He was certain that Major Shani would eventually come around and get him the items on the list. Perhaps he would even offer additional help —he was a man accustomed to dealing with the other side of the fence, but he was also different from other IDF officers in that he was not so immediately dismissive. Rami could see this in the Major's eyes; when he listened he truly listened, took in the information, and weighed the consequences before responding. His apology over following orders and razing Rami's home had seemed sincere.

As he wiped his brow with his handkerchief, Rami convinced himself that this collaboration was in everyone's best interest, including the IDF's, and he allowed himself a small smile. He had no idea if this new relationship with Shani would offer anything more in the future, nor was he thinking that far ahead. For now, all he cared about was getting children off the street and into a better mindset. He didn't want any of them to follow in his son's footsteps and become a face on a placard in the midst of a funeral.

There were those who might argue that even God would not attempt what I have in mind, Rami thought, *but I am determined*. His God was a God of peace and this is where his focus would begin. "Baby steps…" he mumbled, as his feet hurried onward.

When Rami entered his brother's house, he immediately felt relief from the stifling heat outside. As he absently wandered into Imad's bedroom, he noticed something was off; his suitcase had disappeared. He began searching frantically on either side of the bed, then underneath it, then behind the curtains and dresser.

Flinging open the closet door, he found the case standing upright in the far corner. He snatched it out and threw it on the bed, guessing from its weight that it was likely empty. He quickly unfastened the clasps —click-click. They sprung open, revealing exactly what he'd expected. Nothing. He ran back to the closet where he now noticed his clothes were hanging neatly, and furiously began searching again. *Where are they? Where are Hassan's letters?* They were nowhere. His fists clenched. "Lyda! Lyda! Who unpacked my clothes?" The house remained silent.

Making his way to the kitchen, Rami stomped over to the sink and poured a glass of water to calm himself. As he drank, he looked out the window to see Lyda speaking to a man in the back garden. Rami knew of him too well —the man Marwan had mentioned —the man who had warned Imad. He was known as *Moustache*, for the black twin caterpillars that crawled across the space over his mouth and bristled out from under his nose. Certain men in the region used a code name for fear that someone may be listening to their conversations — their plotting.

Rami's eyes narrowed as he watched the two speaking in hushed tones. He paced back and forth struggling with the thought of confronting them and the potential consequences. Just then, *Moustache* reached out, grasped Lyda's hand and placed an envelope in it. She accepted it without comment as he slinked off down the garden path that led to the alley.

A low, guttural growl escaped Rami's throat as he waited for his wife to enter through the back door. When the steel door clanked shut, he snatched the envelope from her hands, startling her.

"We are not accepting money from *those* people! Hassan was *not* part of them!" His eyes bulged, and his spittle travelled the short distance between them.

"You have nothing to say about it! Nothing!" Within the space of seconds, Lyda had become as furious as her husband.

"Nothing?" Rami was incredulous. "I am the man of this house and you will do as I say! You will give this blood money back to those people immediately!"

"What good is the man of the house if he is never *in* the house? There is no man… there isn't even a house anymore!"

She struck him hard in the chest, but he let it go. She was not wrong; their home was gone forever. Still, the fact that she had accepted money from *Moustache* sickened him. "You have already determined the price of Hassan's life?"

"I've determined nothing but that he's gone! Gone!"

Rami's voice rose in pitch and volume. "His name is Hassan! Hassan! Use it when you speak of our son!"

His demand echoed off the walls and faded into the corners of the room, leaving the miserable couple in silence.

"*Hassan* only wanted his father to be home," Lyda said finally.

"I went away to protect you and Hassan. It was the only thing we could do."

"*We* didn't do anything. *You* did all this without even speaking to me. One day you were here and the next day you were gone. How do you think that made me feel?"

"I told you that I had a teaching contract in Romania. I was sure you would understand."

Lyda's fury resurfaced. "Understand what? You told me within the space of an hour and then you were gone for years. You explained nothing! You never speak!"

"Understand that I would have had to work for *them*." He pointed violently in the direction of the garden. Suddenly feeling exposed by their raised voices, he motioned for her to follow him into the bedroom. Once there, Rami shut the door.

"That man is connected to Imad! He is dangerous. You shame us by taking that money!"

Lyda looked startled, her eyes filling with tears. "He said he was a friend of the family. Do you think he... do you think he killed our son?"

Rami felt her horror and tried to calm down. "I don't know, but trust me... I am determined to find out. I just have to find out in my own way... in my own time." His eyes returned to his suitcase. "Now, who unpacked my things?"

Lyda looked confused. "I hung up your clothes. It's impolite to leave your bags out like that in your brother's home."

Marching over to the closet, Rami tore his clothes from the coat hangers and began stuffing them haphazardly into his suitcase. "Leave my things alone! My things are my things and they are not to be touched!"

"But everything is wrinkled. You cannot walk around like that. You have been wearing the same clothes for days! You look like a beggar!"

"Leave – my – things – alone!" Rami shouted, punching his clothes with his fist for emphasis. "I will not ask you again!"

Lyda watched him destroy any semblance of order to his belongings, mixed emotions etched across her fragile features. "Where do you think you are going? Is the only reason I have my husband by my side because they won't let you leave?"

Ignoring her question, Rami returned to the closet and searched the upper shelf for a second time. "Where are they?"

"Where are what?"

"The letters… the letters that were in the suitcase! Where are they?"

Her eyes welling up again, Lyda drifted to the bureau and pulled out the handful of wrinkled envelopes from behind Imad's photograph. "At first, I thought they were from another woman," she confessed, her gaze dropping to the floor in shame. "Then I saw Hassan's handwriting. I didn't know he wrote to you. He didn't tell me."

Rami calmed and took the letters from her hand, placing them carefully back in the suitcase between the mound of clothes. "He kept a lot of secrets." He closed the case and fastened the clasps.

Lyda's eyes hardened. "So that's it? Just like that! You are going to walk out on me again? Doesn't it even occur to you to stay? Do you think of nothing but yourself?"

"We've been through this. You know why I can't stay. Nothing has changed. When the investigation is over, I will return to Bucharest and continue to teach at the university. I will send you money for food and clothes, as I did when Hassan was alive. It has never been about myself! It has always been about you and Hassan. Always! *That* is why I left, and *that* is why I must leave again!"

"You go because you are a coward!"

Rami's eyes flashed. He raised his hand to slap his wife but reeled backwards instead, catching his breath. Grabbing his suitcase, he stormed out of the room leaving Lyda with her hand instinctively held to her cheek, hurt, ashamed and angry.

Once in the living room, Rami realized he had nowhere to go. He desperately wished he could escape, to return to some semblance of normalcy and feel in charge of his life again, but he was stuck here in a home that wasn't his, with a woman whose bitterness seemed to prey on whatever kernel of dignity he had left. Defeated, he tucked his suitcase behind the overstuffed chair in the living room and made his way back outside into the stifling heat.

Chapter   12

The carpet of freshly watered grass added a welcome contrast to the dusty earth surrounding it. *Where there is water there is life*, thought Shani. *And where there is life... joy.* It made him proud to hear the gleeful giggles of his daughters as they played in the garden he had so painstakingly cultivated.

Grabbing a soccer ball, he kicked it to Sally who did nothing when it landed at her feet. He waited for her to kick it back, but she just stood there, as Lissette watched from the swing-set, and Hofit splashed in and out of the wading pool.

"Kick it back to me," he prodded.

"I don't want to, daddy. Kicking balls is not very lady-like," she informed him.

Depends on whose balls, he thought, smiling. His thick eyebrows rose playfully. "Hmmm. Maybe we should've had a boy. Then I would have someone to play football with!" Taunting her about having a brother was a running joke between them. He waited for the reaction of protest, but her mother interrupted.

"Quit teasing her, Ben!" Dalya placed a tray of drinks on the table.

"I'd love to have a little brother," Sally admitted.

Flipping the ball up with a toe lift, Shani caught it in his hands. "Well, I'll tell you what, your mother and I will speak about it tonight and see what we come up with."

He winked at Dalya; and she discretely puckered her lips into a silent "Shhhh!"

Knowing a thing or two about making babies, Lissette flung herself off the swing and grabbed a drink to hide her embarrassment. Hofit and Sally joined her at the table.

Shani was his most content when surrounded by his wife and daughters at his favorite time of the day. The heat was slowly beginning to dwindle, and the radiant red hue of the sun had already begun to fade. A slight breeze picked up making the wet curls on Hofit's head dance, and this added to his serenity.

He sat and slowly sipped the chilled lemonade, which had been sweetened with honey harvested by their neighbor. Dalya had picked the fragrant lemons from a nearby tree that very afternoon, and the oily zest shimmered between the crushed ice in the glass. He felt so lucky to have such a caring woman in his life. He looked at his daughters and felt the same unconditional love. Tossing the ball from his lap, he cleared his scratchy throat. "I want to ask you all a question."

The three girls looked at each other. Shani knew that he had their attention —they were familiar with his more serious tone, as it nearly always had to do with his work. Living in an Israeli settlement had, in many ways, made his children older than their years. Everyone in the region had to remain alert, even when there seemed to be nothing happening, politically or otherwise. They all knew a flare up could happen at any time. That natural suspicion of everything —that wariness and vigilance —had become the basis of survival for all, regardless of age.

"If you were in school and there was a boy in your class who asked to borrow a pencil, and you had one to lend, would you give it to him?"

The girls thought about it, Hofit scrunching up her face in what Shani read as indecision.

"I would," Lissette answered matter-of-factly.

Shani smiled. "Okay. Now, what if he was an Arab boy? A Palestinian?"

The question landed like a brick on the hard earth. No one spoke for a moment but everyone fidgeted as if they wished they were somewhere else. Hofit surprised her parents by piping up first.

"I would."

Her father glanced over at her mother and they shared a smile.

Sally looked annoyed. "What do you know about anything? You don't even go to school yet."

"I will soon. And who cares anyway, he still needs a pencil."

Out of the mouths of babes, thought Shani, as he leaned back in his chair, his decision made.

Chapter 13

At his brother's house, Rami fluttered in and out of the last moments of a dream. He mumbled a word or two and then bolted upright, wide-awake, sweating and breathing heavily. "What... where?" He gradually became aware of his surroundings, and that he'd spent another night asleep in a living room chair —this one less comfortable than his own. He was aching and stiff and his clothes were once again wrinkled. He reached over to the suitcase on the floor beside him and flipped it open to ponder the choice of other crumpled clothes he would wear for the day.

As he stood to dress, Rose entered the living room, shot him a surprised look —an obligatory morning greeting —and then quickly exited. She was a short, round woman with small, dark eyes, and lips that appeared constantly pursed — at least, around Rami. He knew that she was not fond of him. It was obvious that she viewed him as a deserter. She was a distant cousin to Lyda and looked after her as a mother fox looks after her cub... vigilantly and dutifully. The woman didn't miss a beat. Rami could almost admire her if it wasn't for her general lack of imagination and her quickness to judge others so harshly. Still, her pragmatic nature appeared to suit Marwan, and was certainly helping Lyda cope with her grief. For this, Rami was grateful

On his way to his brother's café, Rami passed Rafik and Yasser with several of their friends. They all appeared aimless —seemingly hanging out with no purpose in life, and none forthcoming.

Rami's sadness returned. These lost children so desperately needed something to look forward to. If only Hassan was here now, he would be included in his plan.

When he reached the café, he found Marwan sitting on one of his patio chairs fanning himself. Sweat trickled down his neck nonetheless. With the exception of one customer the day was quiet again, which seemed to have become the norm. Usually, it was the heat that kept people indoors without much to do but wait out the hot winds. Now, the village had become substantially quieter since the bombing.

Rami knew that the decline in patrons didn't really bother his brother since he did not rely solely on the café for his living. Many people in the region did whatever they could to make ends meet. No one person was a master of one thing, but a dabbler in many. For Marwan, the café was his cooking haven, his office, and his distribution center. If someone needed something, Marwan would get it for him or her —for a price, of course. Like his wife, he was pragmatic by nature, believing that anything more prosperous than his day-to-day existence was simply a pipe dream, but also acknowledging that no opportunity should be overlooked.

On seeing Rami, Marwan poured a cup of coffee and placed it in front of him.

"You look terrible!" -

"I am fine. Thank you for your concern." Rami looked over at the sole customer sitting in the corner of the patio. She appeared to be listening.

"I keep telling you that you should eat something. Let me make one of my famous French omelets." Marwan was relentless.

Rami smiled. "You and your French Omelets. Don't trouble yourself." He nodded discreetly in the customer's direction. "Who is that? She looks familiar."

"Christine Cooper... the journalist."

Rami looked at his brother reproachfully. "Ah, now I see why you invited me for a coffee this morning."

"What?" Marwan said, feigning innocence. "She is just another customer."

"Who tips well, I presume."

"Who tips well... yes. I don't have too many of them around anymore... as you can see."

Marwan motioned for Christine to come over. She sat across from Rami and placed her half-finished cup of coffee on the table. She was a tall woman with cropped auburn hair and slate blue eyes that appeared to warm in color when she smiled. Her beauty was outdoorsy, natural, honest, and completely played down by her choice of simple, loose-fitting clothes.

"Good morning, Doctor Amar, I really appreciate you…"

"This really isn't a good time," Rami interrupted. He vaguely recalled having heard that she had won awards for her abilities. He had no intention of letting his son's story be another notch in her belt.

Christine was quiet for a moment. It was obvious that she was a seasoned journalist accustomed to being rebuked a million times. Still, she always managed to get her story. She bit her lip and looked directly into his eyes. "This really isn't a good time. That's what I always tell my wife when she calls." An awkward moment, and then she continued. "When I see her number come up on my phone, I avoid her… my own wife! It's not that I don't *want* to talk to her, it's just that it's easier now if I don't."

Rami looked at her, unsure of where she was going, but for the moment, she had his attention.

"I don't know what to say anymore because we would always talk about our son, Jack. But those conversations ended when he drowned."

Rami felt the stab of his own loss. "I am sorry to hear that. My deepest condolences."

"Thank you, but... that's not why I'm telling you this. I'm telling you this because I want you to know that I understand loss... the loss of a child."

Rami reached for his cup and softly blew before he sipped. It was something to do to fill another awkward moment.

"Ironically enough it was because of a fence. The neighbor bought it to put around his pool and there it was rolled up in the corner of his yard waiting to go up." Christine paused shaking her head. "It's the law, you know. Where we live, if you have a swimming pool you must surround it with a fence for safety." Her words hung in the air like a mist until she swallowed sharply and continued, her voice cracking.

"You turn around and they are suddenly walking and talking; you turn around again and they're gone."

Rami listened more attentively now, not because he was adept at listening to other people's pain and nodding his head by rote; and not because he didn't want to appear rude while this woman bared her soul. She had his attention simply because her voice had cracked —her grief was still raw.

"But the loss of my son is not the story here, and I realize you may never be able to speak to me about the loss of yours." Christine was aligning herself with Rami and he knew it, but he nodded and let her continue.

"In my case, I feel incredibly guilty because my work allows me to escape the daily reminders of our son's death; unlike Melinda, my wife, who is forced to relive the ordeal every time she looks out of our bedroom window and into our neighbor's back yard. It's not fair to her."

Rami stared at the journalist unwilling to interrupt, but at the same time, feeling uncomfortable about hearing such intimate details. *People spend lifetimes together without revealing such things*, he thought.

"I guess I just want you to know that *your* story of loss is very important to me; I will treat it with the upmost of care and respect."

"Ms. Cooper, what do you want from me exactly?"

"I want you to share your story with the world —tell us who Hassan was, and how you and your wife are dealing with the aftermath of all of this."

Rami suddenly stiffened. "Please do not harass my wife!"

"No, of course not. But please don't think of my interest in covering your story as harassment. This has affected so many people. I just want you to be able to share your side of this tragedy —talk about how you are feeling."

Rami took a deep breath. "You will leave my wife out of this. She will not be discussed. As for *my* feelings… when I know what they are, and how to articulate them, I will let you know."

"Thank you! That is all I ask." Christine pushed back her chair to stand, and then stopped. "Is that a promise?"

"No, it is not!"

Rami's response took her aback. As another awkward silence floated over them, she stood up to leave. "Thank you for your time, Dr. Amar. Your brother knows how to reach me." She smiled self-consciously, placed some cash on the table, and walked away.

Rami looked at his brother, displeased at him for putting him on the spot. Marwan shrugged his shoulders in a "What?" gesture.

"You know exactly what!"

Marwan shrugged again and pocketed the cash on the table. "By the way, the boxes by the counter are your school supplies. The Israeli's dumped them here yesterday. That Corporal Cohen is a *joy*! Still, he bought a few waters for his soldiers when he saw business was slow, so I minded my manners." Marwan grinned.

Thrilled that Shani had delivered even though he had never promised to, Rami looked over and saw the boxes had been opened. "Yes, and thank you for going through them."

"Happy to oblige, though I don't know why you didn't just come to me for the items."

"For a price, my brother? These were free," Rami joked. "Besides, you are helping me enough with a place to stay."

Marwan's demeanor became serious. "Be careful about interacting with the Israeli's. People will think you're a collaborator."

"Don't be crazy! The Israeli's destroyed my house remember? Me working for them would be the last thing anyone with a reasonable mind would be thinking."

"Reasonable minds are in short supply in this part of the world," Marwan reminded him. "Anyway, how do you plan on getting this stuff up to the school?"

"On your ass of course!"

Rami and Marwan looked over to the tired donkey tied up behind the café. Rami whistled to the boys on the street and motioned them over.

Marwan smiled and acceptingly shook his head. "I think I know exactly what you hope to accomplish."

"I'm not so hard to figure out." Rami turned to Rafik and Yasser as they approached. "I need your help." They didn't answer, but instead just looked down at their feet. "I will pay you," Rami added.

Their heads perked up in unison. "What do we have to do?" Rafik asked.

"Simple. You have to help me clean up the school so that classes can begin."

"How much will we get paid?"

Rami admired the boy's acumen. He nodded to Marwan who brought over two cold drinks and placed them down in front of the boys.

"Cold drinks for one, and beyond that… something you cannot put a price on."

Yasser grabbed the drink, but Rafik stuffed his hands in his pockets and persisted. "But if you could come close, what would the price be?"

Rami thought about it for a moment. "What it pays leaves the value up to you."

"What is it? What is it?" Yasser could hardly contain his excitement. Rafik merely shook his head in frustration.

Marwan lingered behind the boys amused by the exchange.

"Knowledge!" Rami revealed with the flair of a magician. The boys recoiled in unison. "Knowledge?"

"Yes, knowledge. An Education!"

They both exhaled like deflating balloons. "We already have plenty of that!" Rafik said defiantly.

"Do you?" Rami asked.

"Yes we do!" Rafik stood his ground.

"And where do you get it? Across the street in the dirt?"

"At home. My parents teach me!" Yasser quickly finished the contents of the bottle and placed it back on the table with a satisfied burp.

"Is that why I see you out here playing in the dirt every day?"

"We're busy anyway." Rafik tried to pull Yasser away.

SMACK!

"Ouch!"

Marwan had cuffed Rafik on the nape of his neck. "Busy doing what?" he asked, all amusement gone from his eyes. "You'll go help clean up that school and then you will go *to* that school and learn something. That goes for the both of you."

Yasser looked back down at his shoes while Rafik remained angry and silent.

'What?" Marwan dared him, "You have something to say?" The silence was deafening. "I didn't think so!" Marwan headed back to his counter. "And bring all of your lazy cousins hanging around the newsstand all day." He shot Rami a wink and began wiping the counter down.

Yasser piped up first. "What will my parents say?"

"They'll say go to school, learn something… from the best!" Marwan resumed his cleaning and began humming a tune that had been in his head all morning.

Rami watched the boys saunter away, before looking back at his brother. "Was that really necessary? I wanted them to come through their own volition."

"You would have waited an eternity."

"Still, did you have to hit him?"

"What hit? It was a tap," returned Marwan smiling. "Besides, you had lost them. They needed a stern hand to steer them back."

"I suppose," Rami replied. "Some things you were always better at than me."

Marwan waved his brother's comment off without breaking his rhythm.

Chapter 14

Further down the road, Christine had made her way back to her cameraman, Greg. When she saw the interaction between Rami and the two boys, she quickly jotted down a few notes in her notebook. "I wonder what that's about," she said, more to herself than Greg.

She watched as the boys slowly sauntered off, their small statures bringing her back to the day she'd received the call about her son. It was one of those sticky days in Beirut, and she had been working on a story about the abuse of domestic migrant workers within the more affluent regions of Lebanon. It was not a story she would normally be assigned, but she was covering it because it was to be a major piece in a documentary series for her network. Workers from poorer countries, who traveled from places like Sri Lanka and Pakistan to seek work, were being exposed to mistreatment without the protection of citizenry. Human rights violations were a global problem, and the Middle East was no exception.

Christine remembered that her white linen shirt had stuck to her like glue that day despite the majestic Mediterranean breeze making its way inland off the coast. Beyond feeling overheated, her gut was agitated —an internal tugging that had nothing to do with the migrant story. She was unsettled; her instincts were tingling —a feeling of foreboding making her anxious —but she couldn't figure out why, nor could she shake it. *Then the call came.*

"Hi, baby!" Christine had answered in her usual loving way. She'd missed her wife and was happy to see her name pop up on her screen. But Melinda didn't respond. "Hello?" Christine repeated. "Mel?"

"Chris..." Melinda's voice was so cracked and restrained it was barely recognizable. Then,

Christine heard the most heartbreaking wail. It was the sound of uncontrollable grief —a sound she had never heard from Melinda before in all the years they'd known each other.

After a few moments of calming Melinda down, Christine finally received the heart-wrenching news.

"Jack drowned," Melinda whimpered.

Christine would always remember the feeling of becoming instantly chilled to the bone on the hottest day of the year. When she called her boss, Kaye, and gave him the news, she was immediately released from her assignment. There was no question; she could take as much time as she needed.

"Come back only when you are absolutely ready," he had said.

The flight home had been excruciatingly long. As over-tired as she was, Christine could not close her eyes, let alone sleep. She wanted to scream, *'How? How could this happen?'* Her heart ached for Jack, for Melinda, and for herself. Her wife's broken voice kept replaying over and over again in her head.

She had never heard Melinda sound so helpless, and she would never be able to forget it.

She shook the memory off as Greg passed her a bottle of water. "You need to stay hydrated," he said firmly. He cared about her and she found this comforting.

"Thank you," she replied, sipping intermittently and fanning herself with her notebook. She sat down on the edge of a wall and continued watching the doctor and his brother, who were now alone. "Where did the boys go?"

"No idea," replied Greg who was fiddling with his camera.

A dusty taxi rolled by, and, once again, Christine's thoughts drifted to Melinda. The cab from the airport had dropped her off at their home, and she had taken in several deep breaths before walking up to the door. The driveway and the road around the house were filled with cars she recognized.

When she entered, she found the house filled with parents, siblings, and other family members. Even a few neighbors had dropped by, bringing food and offering long embraces and condolences.

"There are no words that exist that could make sense of such a tragedy," someone had said.

"The best thing that anyone could hope for is that they go before their children," someone else said.

"Getting over it is so unimaginable at this point in time that one thinks they will never heal. But healing will come."

Christine had drifted from one room to another, sporting exhausted, unfocused eyes —all her functions on automatic —until she found Melinda outside on the patio away from all of the well-meaning platitudes. The two of them locked eyes and embraced tightly as they both sobbed.

"Where are you?" Asked Greg, bringing her back to the present.

Christine shrugged and turned her attention back to the café. As Marwan wandered away to attend to a new customer, Rami appeared to retreat into his own world. Even from a distance, Christine could feel the energy around him retract. She knew his state of mind so intimately —the need to withdraw juxtaposing the need to keep moving in order to stay alive. The moment *she* stopped, even for an instant, the pain would come flooding back, making it harder to move again. Rami was no different. There they were, two people in pain. They should be talking to one another — consoling one another —not for the story, but for each other. She felt a pang of remorse for attempting to exploit the Doctor's feelings. The story was secondary. She just wanted to be his friend. Maybe she wanted this for herself —or maybe she wanted to be there for *him*. Maybe it would help them both. But then again... maybe not

"I'm gonna go edit some stuff," Greg said. Nothing. Greg tried again. "Christine?" Christine turned her head towards him still not fully attentive.

"Huh?"

"I'm going to go cut some stuff and upload," Greg repeated.

"Yeah, all right, but let me see it before it goes."

"Of course, boss! Like always." Greg smiled, grabbed his camera off the wall, and walked away.

Christine and Greg had become close over the years; they were more than collaborators... they were friends. She knew that he understood her. He had witnessed the *Before Christine* —the dedicated professional with integrity and a great sense of the story. And, he'd stuck by the *After Christine* —the shattered professional, still with integrity and a great sense of story, but who was struggling every day with her pain. She wondered if the *Before Christine* would ever resurface. Thank goodness Greg was a patient colleague.

Chapter 15

Rami coaxed the overloaded donkey up the uneven path towards the school. *This ass is as stubborn as its owner*, he thought. He wondered if Marwan had whispered in its ear to give him an especially hard time. The slow beast kept stopping every few steps and looking at Rami with distaste. Rafik and Yasser, each struggling with their own boxes, were of no help urging it along. There was a chorus of complaints the whole way up that was barely discernable from boy to donkey.

As they looked down at the playing field, they took in the giant boulder.

"That thing is huge," Rami noted.

"When the Jews were shelling, it got knocked loose and rolled down from way up there." Rafik pointed to the peak of the hill behind the school. "It's as if they *wanted* to ruin our football game too!"

When they arrived at the dilapidated school, the sound of the boxes dropping to the ground was accompanied by over-exaggerated moans and groans from the boys. *That was likely the hardest ten minutes they have ever worked in their lives*, Rami thought, quietly chuckling to himself. He wiped his brow with his handkerchief and blotted the sweat behind his ears. The sun was relentless and he welcomed the cooler yet musty interior of the single-story building. He hopped over the broken glass and debris inside, while the boys perched on the outside steps.

Looking around, he quickly cleared a corner where they could stack the boxes and instructed the boys to remove the load from the donkey. Having barely sat down, Rafik and Yasser cursed themselves for having been talked into such an escapade and leered at Rami.

"Don't give me that look. This will be over before you know it." Rami scolded.

The boys begrudgingly untied the load, grabbed two brooms, and shuffled into the classroom for the messy cleanup.

Over the next few days, Rami, Rafik and Yasser removed the debris, repaired and painted the walls, erected the blackboard, and wiped away the grime from the desks and chairs. When they were finished, Rami inspected the results and was pleased. He decided that school was now in session and told the boys to take a seat as he passed them pencils and notebooks.

As their first class began, he scratched a few words onto the blackboard and then turned to face his new students. Their bored expressions clearly indicated that they would rather be outside throwing rocks at bottles, or kicking around a football.

"Forget about everything you have been taught. Just for a few minutes. Everything!" He instructed.

The two boys looked at each other and shrugged.

"Why is it that we Palestinians do not have freedom?" Rami knew that whatever their answer, it would likely be misguided.

Yasser put his hand up, but when Rafik glared at him he lowered it timidly.

"Yasser, don't be afraid to speak!" Rami encouraged.

"Because the Jews will not let us!"

Rami sighed deeply. This was going to be a long, uphill battle.

"Why does someone drive a car filled with explosives into a building, or send someone rigged up into the nearest group of Israelis?

"To kill them!" Rafik waved his fist over his head. "To kill as many of them as we can!"

Rami moved closer to the boys, and in a slow, deliberate voice asked, "What purpose does that serve? Does it get you freedom? By killing all of those innocent people, do the occupiers go away and leave you alone?"

"No, they come with more soldiers and kill us!" Yasser sat up straighter in his seat, proud that he had answered correctly.

"Then what? We send another bomber — another young man or woman to be killed? What happens then?"

"Then they attack us again!" Rafik's snarled.

"So, what is the point? What purpose does it all serve?"

The boys looked to each other but neither had an answer.

"Nothing! It accomplishes nothing!" Rami shook his head. "So, isn't it time to change our approach? If I am trying to knock down a wall by banging my head against it, and that doesn't work, I must change my method. Wouldn't you agree?" Rami could see uncertainty in Rafik and Yasser's eyes. He'd struck a nerve. "It's the same with the cycle of violence that happens here. What would you do? What approach would *you* take to stop the killing?"

"I don't know, what would *you* do?" Rafik answered.

"What I would do is not the point of this lesson."

"Then what *is* the point of this lesson?"

Rami sat on the edge of Rafik's desk and spoke calmly and deliberately. "The point of this lesson is to teach you to think for yourself. If you wish to knock down a wall, and banging your head against it is futile, then obviously your method needs modification. Agreed?"

"These words are too big for me," Yasser complained.

"Which?"

"Few-something and Mod-a-fiction. What do they mean?"

"The first word is futile. It means pointless… unsuccessful… ineffective. The second is mod-*i*-fication. It means to change something… to alter or readjust a method that doesn't work." Rami pointed to the blackboard. "I've written them down for you."

Yasser looked at the board and then opened his notebook and began copying down the words. *Great*, thought Rami, *they're already starting to learn.*

"I knew that already," Rafik bragged.

"Ok, good. Then let's start at the beginning," Rami took a deep breath and returned to the front of the classroom. Picking up a piece of chalk, he turned and looked at the boys. "First, we must decide what *goals* we want to achieve. For example?"

"Not getting killed," answered Rafik quickly.

"Perfect," replied Rami. "Then, we need to decide what methods need to be *modified* to achieve that goal." He smiled at Yasser, and then turned and began tapping on the blackboard with the dusty chalk.

Chapter 16

Shani sat on the examination table waiting for the doctor to come back with the results of his test. The disposable paper cover crinkled and crackled every time he shifted his weight. The sound unnerved him; it seemed louder than it needed to be. To calm himself, he tried to concentrate on the din that found its way under the door from the rest of clinic. He watched expectantly as the shadows approached and then disappointingly passed by.

He had been chastising himself since Dr. Amar's brusque diagnosis. The signs were so gradual he hadn't noticed them at first. Yet, those around him did. "You haven't been eating," Dalya kept telling him. Why had he ignored her? For fear of the truth —that he was not invincible? He recalled the coffee at Dr. Amar's house filling his empty stomach; his difficulty swallowing; and the nagging cough that kept him up at night. When the Doctor told him to look into it, his symptoms finally had weight. Dr. Amar was trained to see things most people did not, and his instincts —his good healing nature —would not let him withhold that information, even from his enemy, even from the man who'd destroyed his home. Shani had to respect a man with that kind of integrity.

A shadow lingered outside for a moment and then the door swung open. Shani could see from Doctor Edelman's downturned lips that the news was not good.

"This is the footage from the endoscopy," Doctor Edelman said, turning his tablet around to show Shani the image on the screen.

A microscopic camera had been used to look down Shani's throat. The doctor pressed play, and Shani saw what looked like a wet pink tunnel being channeled.

"There!" Doctor Edelman paused the image and enlarged it with a swipe of his finger. "That's the beginning of a small tumor on your oropharynx."

Shani stared, dumbfounded. "Cancer?" He mumbled.

"Cancer," the doctor repeated. "But it seems we caught it early, before it got away from us."

"Cancer," Shani said a second time, as if staring at the image was enough to make it go away. "Am I going to die?"

"Someday, yes. But hopefully not because of this."

"You can cut it out?"

"We can do a micro laser removal, and hopefully that will be the end of it."

"Can you do it today?"

"No, but we can schedule it for this week." Dr. Edelman saw Shani's disappointment and added, "You'll be in and out the same day. And you get to eat ice cream afterwards."

"Perfect, my girls love ice cream!"

Doctor Edelman placed the tablet down and put his hand on Shani's shoulder. "Ben, I haven't seen you here for *too* long. It's your good fortune that you decided to come in for a checkup. If you'd left it much longer... well, we'd be having a different conversation. Consider yourself lucky." He patted Shani's back reassuringly and turned to leave. "I assume any day we can book the surgery will work for you?"

"Yes, of course. But please call my mobile, not the house."

The doctor looked confused for a moment, and then nodded sympathetically and walked out.

Shani decided he didn't need to tell Dalya or the girls just yet. *Why make them worry if there's nothing to worry about?* He stood up feeling both anxious and relieved. He needed to find a way to thank Dr. Amar without it getting in the way of the investigation —without feeling he owed the man a debt.

Chapter 17

Rami could no longer tell what was suffocating Lyda more, the heat or her grief. Concerned, he moved back into the bedroom to keep an eye on her. Upon first light, as her eyes fluttered open, he watched Lyda's anxiety take hold. She would grasp at her chest and sit up struggling to take in air before calming herself enough to begin her day. When she rose, she moved around slowly and stiffly as if her joints were partially fused. Sleep, when she could surrender to it, was her only refuge.

For Rami, not even sleep could relieve his pain, but now he had something to occupy his time during the day, and this helped him forget his anguish intermittingly until the light in the sky dwindled and dusk set in. During this time, he and

Lyda existed in their own little world —their mantra; *I am alive; I must move forward; I must bear this unspeakable agony* —sitting on their hearts. These were the loneliest moments for them both, and only those who had experienced such loss could understand.

Lyda's crying was unpredictable often beginning without provocation. When she looked out of the window, her mind went elsewhere as her eyes became transfixed —glued to something a million miles away. When she reemerged from her daze, she was often confused as to how she came to be at the window in the first place. She appeared to eat without tasting, to drink without quenching her thirst, and to hear without listening. She had truly become a ghost.

Rami recalled Lyda once telling him that she had felt the safest in her father's lap with her head nestled into his chest and his moustache tickling her forehead as he kissed it. At that time, she also admitted that she had felt a calming stillness when in Rami's arms, which came close to that feeling of protection from her father. But that confession seemed a lifetime ago. It had been ages since they'd spoken so intimately to each other —ages since they'd really looked into each other's eyes as partners, lovers, man and wife. Rami knew that Lyda loved him, and he loved her, but was love enough to get them through this heartbreak? It seemed to Rami that courage was also needed —the courage to breathe —to put one foot in front of the other and dare to move forward —the courage to mourn together as a couple.

"A parent should never outlive their child," Lyda said suddenly one morning, as she stared at the sunlight splayed across on the ceiling above Imad's bed. To Rami's surprise, she rolled onto her side, and, for the first time since his arrival, looked at him without contempt. "It hurts too much."

Rami nodded in agreement aware that Lyda's sudden statement was a good sign. He knew that the hole created by her grief could never be filled; but she would slowly become more accustomed to that void, and other ways of existing would gradually emerge. For now, Lyda needed to do something... anything. There wasn't much in her daily life to occupy her time.

Sliding out of bed, Lyda slipped on her cotton housecoat and made her way to the kitchen. Rami followed and watched her go through her usual morning ritual of standing at the stove and adding rich aromatic grounds of Turkish coffee into a pot of water. After stirring in a teaspoon of sugar, she removed the pot from the heat just at the boiling-over point, and then roiled it for a few minutes before sitting down at the table. As the coffee settled her mind wandered away again, her face drawn and pensive, until she finally poured the dark liquid into a small, white cup, and watched the edges froth up and spin around the rim.

Lyda was an expert at *coffee reading*, an art that had been passed down by her mother, and one that was a long-standing custom in Beit Jbal. When the coffee was poured, how it framed the cup and the amount of froth, all carried meaning for her. When the liquid was cool enough, she sipped thoughtfully until all that remained was the earthy residue. Swirling the dregs in the cup with one hand, she turned it upside down onto the saucer and then passed it to Rami.

"It's bad luck to read my own cup," she said, her dark eyes pressing him on. Rami had never read a cup before —it had never interested him much — but her gaze was so insistent, he could not protest.

He knew that Lyda had always relied more on the spontaneous impressions that came to her when interpreting the grainy patterns, as opposed to something more studied and exact. It had been years since he had watched her do this, and the fact that she was turning to it now was perhaps another sign that she was at last stepping back into the world.

Turning over the cup, Rami said the first thing that came into his mind as he looked at the cluster of grounds… "Children!" He turned the cup around and said confidently, "I see children! You're going to contribute to, and support, the children in the village. You're going to help me change things… one child at a time."

Lyda's eyes widened; a kernel of hope seeded in her curious gaze.

Chapter 18

That afternoon, Rami sat at Marwan's café scanning the pages of a newspaper. His eyes darted across the articles, his lips moving inaudibly before he snapped his hands together to turn the page. He repeated the process page after page —eyes scanning, snap, scan.

"There are contradicting reports from witnesses. Some say they heard him yell "Allah", while others say it sounded more like "Amar" or "Omar." Rami looked up at Marwan. "Do you know anything about this?"

"I have heard these things as well, but it's impossible to know the truth." Marwan restocked the cooler with drinks.

"Hassan was not that religious. I mean, I taught him to respect Islam, to practice it if he wanted to, but he never expressed much interest. So, I let him be."

"Obviously he changed while you were gone."

Rami glared at Marwan indignantly. "I haven't been gone that long! And, I know my son. I raised him. I have letters from him. I know my son!"

Marwan sighed, walked over to Rami, and pulled up a chair. His brow pinched as he took in a deep breath.

"It's impossible to know the truth", he repeated quietly, putting his hand on his brother's shoulder.

Rami was not convinced of Marwan's lack of knowledge and pressed on. "You are completely unaware of any group Hassan may have been a part of? Anyone he might have connected with?"

Marwan shook his head.

"It seems strange that you know everything that is going on around here yet you have heard nothing about this?"

"How many times do I have to tell you? I've heard nothing!"

Rami folded the paper and set it down on the table. "What about Imad? How is my nephew?"

"My son is the same as when you left. Alive, thank God! But a ghost nonetheless."

"I need to speak to him."

"You know that is difficult." Marwan shook his head again, his expression darkening.

"Nonetheless, I want to speak to him. I'm certain *he* knows something," Rami insisted.

"He doesn't know anything! Leave him out of this!"

Rami eyed his brother suspiciously. It wasn't like him to be so explosive. He asked again. "Did he have anything to do with it?"

Marwan stood up refusing to answer, and Rami stood to face him. "Did he have anything to do with it, Marwan?"

"No!"

A long silence drifted between them. Rami sat back down dissatisfied and picked up his paper. "Set up a meeting, brother," he growled, without looking up.

Rami attempted to flip through the paper again, but his thoughts remained on Imad, and the memory of *that night* came back to him. He remembered the joy of being Beit Jbal's only Doctor —of being trusted and loved and needed by everyone in his community. During his many years in the village, he was able to make a decent, quiet living for his family. And then, *that night* happened, beginning with the pounding on the door that had startled him out of deep and peaceful sleep.

The Israeli military had been searching door to door for a kidnapped soldier. Lyda and Rami were sure it was nothing more than a quick routine check, so Lyda rolled over indifferent, while Rami rose to answer. When he opened the door, he was shocked to find a group of masked, armed men standing on the stoop.

"Get dressed and grab your medical bag! You're coming with us!" the leader ordered.

Rami did as he was told, making sure not to disturb his family. When he returned to the door, he was blindfolded and dragged away into the darkness, while Hassen and Lyda were still asleep in their beds.

As they guided him into a small brick factory, Rami could smell the cool, damp concrete mixed with the dust that had accumulated over the years. He shuffled his feet along the gritty floor to assure safe passage, his heart pounding. Once they were inside a warmer, quieter room, his blindfold was removed. He recoiled at what he saw.

A young Israeli soldier was tied to a chair, his shirt drenched in blood; it oozed out of his nose and the gashes on his head. His eyes were swollen from the beating he'd endured, and there was a visible depression in his forehead possibly made by the butt of a rifle.

Rami ran over to the young man and set down his bag. As he triaged the damage, the man's eyes, terrified and exhausted, pleaded for help. Rami pulled his penlight from his pocket and checked the man's pupils. Opening his bag, he searched for sterile gauze and began cleaning out the deep wounds as gently as possible, but his patient cried out when he carefully turned his head to examine the depression.

Rami turned violently toward the men standing around him. "What have you done to him?"

"We introduced ourselves… one by one," sneered the leader, whose voice was tight and coarse.

"He needs to get to a hospital! His skull is fractured!"

"Not until he tells me what I need to know!"

Rami's eyes narrowed. "And what will he be able to tell you? He's just a kid!" He stared into the leader's cold, dark eyes.

"Someone is collaborating with the Israelis, and I need to know who. You need to fix him up — surgically if need be — so that I can keep him talking."

Rami immediately began packing his bag. "I heal people; I do not harm them!" He tried to leave, but one of the men blocked his exit.

"Tell your man to get out of my way!" Rami snarled.

The leader walked toward him. "I cannot do that," he said, ice hanging from every word.

Now that he was closer, Rami was certain he could make out a thick moustache beneath the man's makeshift cotton mask. Rami shook his head. Was this really happening? He looked around the room at the other masked men. One of them averted his gaze and receded further into the shadows. Rami's heart sank. Could one of the men be his nephew? It was certainly possible. His body became rigid. "What are you going to do, shoot me?" He stood his ground, his eyes unyielding.

The leader was unmoved. "I can have a butcher do this or a doctor. Your choice."

"I will not be that doctor! Not today, or any other day!"

"Suit yourself, but you're not going anywhere!" The leader walked over to the terrified soldier and placed a hand on his shoulder. "You are either going to simply watch, or you are going to patch him up." He pulled a pair of rusty pliers from his pocket and handed it to the man next to him, who in turn grabbed the soldier's left hand.

Rami's stomach turned. "Torture doesn't work! If the man doesn't know anything, how can he tell you anything but lies?"

Ignoring Rami, the leader began bombarding the soldier with questions. When the soldier couldn't answer, the henchman ripped out one of the young man's fingernails.

"STOP! STOP!" Heartsick and nauseated, Rami had no choice. Kneeling beside the dying man, he gently cleaned and bandaged his horrific wounds. With the exception of losing Hassan, *that night* would remain the longest and most excruciating of any in his memory.

As Rami sat in the café aimlessly turning the pages of the paper, he could still see the fear in the young soldier's bloodied eyes and hear the echoes of his screaming. He shuddered, remembering that it was the next morning when he'd left his wife and son so abruptly, without much discussion. He'd simply told them that a friend had managed to secure him a teaching post at the School of Medicine in Romania. He kissed them both goodbye, but could not look

Lyda in the eyes. He felt he would crack if he did. He had no intention of implicating his family in the ordeal with the IDF soldier, and he could not, would not, be a part of such heinous acts —acts that revolted him to his core. He had to go. There was no other choice.

Rami shook himself back to the present realizing that it served no one to return to that night and its sickening consequences. Doing so was like ripping the scab off a wound. He decided that if he caught himself remembering that place, he would shake it off and redirect his train of thought. It was bad enough that the event still permeated his dreams and disrupted his sleep.

He looked over at his brother who had become sullen and distant as he washed the pans in the sink and noisily returned them to the rack. Though he would never admit it, Marwan had a certain hidden pride in his son's courage and convictions, even if he didn't agree with Imad's methods. This was vastly different from how Rami felt about his nephew. Though Imad had a magnetic personality, Rami felt he had always lacked empathy for others. He could be manipulative, unpredictable, and ruthless, all of which was heightened when he became involved with extremists. And, there was also the question of whether Imad had been there on *that night*, something that had sat with Rami ever since.

Rami knew that a meeting with Imad was virtually impossible. So, when Rami told Marwan to set one up, it was with the understanding that all Marwan could do was leave word for his son with some of the local radicals. Stories had been circulating for years about Imad's ability to recruit. The word on the street was that he was so compelling just meeting him could push a young man into offering himself up for whatever cause Imad was advocating. In a world where frustrations festered, lack of opportunity was the norm, and the environment seemed endlessly oppressive, it did not take much to redirect some young man's aggression.

It had crossed Rami's mind that his nephew might have swayed Hassan, who had been one of his many admirers for years. But, counter to his character, Imad had been unusually protective of his cousin. Had this changed? Rami needed to know if he was involved in Hassan's fate, but he was afraid of what the answer might be.

The next few weeks in the classroom proved to be more grueling than Rami had predicted. What had started out as a class for two had quickly become a class for many. Boys of all ages and all levels of education were represented in the small makeshift space.

Rafik and Yasser had been good ambassadors for the school's opening. However, everyone's one-sided thinking was so ingrained that Rami had to muster up all of his resolve to remain patient, and not get angry or show frustration with what they had learned at home and on the streets. Instead, he found a way to slowly chip away at the day's lessons, which often evolved into philosophical clouds that would quickly dissipate from his student's short attention spans.

Rami quickly realized that he could not expect the boys to grasp the geographical and political complications that affected their daily lives when even adults had a difficult time fathoming their region. The West Bank was simply littered with too many struggles. Inhabitants did not feel the heat increase daily, but instead awakened one day to find that it was, in fact, too hot. It burned the nerves. It boiled the blood. It put everyone on edge. In the neighborhoods and out in the fields, in the streets and the back alleys, anger and frustration festered in a way that was unique to the area. And so, it was with the political weather —the wear and tear of cultural hostilities and intolerance. Every evening when Rami returned to the house and laid his tired body beside Lyda, he reminded himself that everything worthwhile took time.

It was almost a month before Rami felt he was starting to make a difference. One morning, as he put down his chalk to begin teaching, he found the classroom bustling with curiosity and questions, debates and discussions about the previous day's class when he had focused on the word *escalation*. He had used an argument that had erupted between Rafik and Yasser as an example of escalation, and then applied it in a broader context.

He waited patiently and listened to the boys' chatter, interjecting now and again to steer the conversations to something productive. "Look for solutions to prevent things from escalating," he reminded them. "Hone your arguments with reason not emotion. Put yourself in the other person's shoes."

By the end of the day, the buzzing wasp nest of boys hovered around him as they all walked back into town. When they questioned, they learned; and this was what Rami wanted them to do —to question everything —to think for themselves. As they neared the village square, the boys gradually peeled off in their own direction leaving Rami in the loneliness of the aftermath. Rami soon found himself walking in the direction of his brother's café.

Marwan anticipated his brother's first question before Rami could open his mouth. "I have heard nothing yet."

"Did you make contact?" Rami persisted.

"I sent a message."

"And…?"

"And when I hear something, I will let you know."

Rami let out a frustrated sigh as he paced between the chairs while Marwan continued to wipe off the tabletops. When Marwan was finished, he approached Rami and lowered his voice.

"You know he has to be very cautious. They are always looking for him. When he feels it is safe to meet, he will let us know." Rami eyed him suspiciously. Marwan looked hurt. "Do not give me that look. Mother looked at me that way when she didn't believe what I was telling her." He walked back to the fridge, popped open a cola, and brought it to his brother. "Now sit down and let me make you my famous French omelet!"

"Marwan, how many times are you going to offer me an omelet?"

"Until you say yes."

"Well, today is not the day, brother. I really should get home to Lyda. We have barely spoken since I began teaching, but we have argued over one or two silly things, which is probably a good sign."

"My wife tells me Lyda walks around the house like a ghost. I understand of course. The loss of a child is the most difficult thing I can imagine happening to anyone." A silence settled between them. "I may soon feel the same way about my own son. It's only a matter of time I fear."

Rami looked up at his brother concerned, having never heard him express such weary resignation. "It is a merciless part of the world we live in," he replied.

They both lingered on that thought as a warm summer wind whistled up from the north. Then, the stillness of the evening was interrupted by gunfire in the distance. They almost didn't notice.

Chapter 19

A few days later, Rami sat fidgeting at his usual table at the café. He was getting more and more impatient, and cast steely glances at his brother to accentuate his displeasure. Marwan simply shrugged. "There is no way he will come near us with all this heat around."

"Does he know I am waiting?" Rami asked.

"He knows, he knows." Marwan's eyes drifted across the street. Rami looked to see what had caught his attention and saw a short, stalky man dragging Yasser by his wrist towards the cafe. The man stopped at Rami's table, glaring at him, while Rami looked up clearly uncomfortable by his proximity.

"I am Ahmed Assaf... this boy's father. Are you his teacher?"

"I am." Rami peered around him to see Yasser's flushed cheeks. "And how is my young student, today?"

Yasser looked away.

"Answer the man!" his father demanded.

"I'm fine, sir,' Yasser replied faintly.

"Good, good." Rami turned his attention back to his father. "What can I do for you, sir?"

"I do not approve of you teaching my son that the Jews are better than us!"

"What are you talking about?" Rami was dumbfounded.

"How can you teach such lies?"

"That is not what I teach!" Rami looked over at Yasser again who still had not made eye contact with him. "I teach the children about equality... about tolerance."

Rami had hoped this day would never come. He'd had a hard time getting through to the boys, but once he did they began to flourish, even take pride in their learning. He expected that enthusiasm to eventually extend to their home life; that —like every child who thinks he knows something that no one else does —each student would share his newfound knowledge with his family, and this would spark a healthy debate. But the anger of Yasser's father crushed Rami's optimism. Narrow-minded fathers like Yasser's demanded adherence to ridged and outmoded beliefs. He was a perfect example of why these boys initially thought the way they did. They were tainted by the anger and prejudice that prevailed in the minds of their patriarch —attitudes that trickled down through to their wives and children, and that were resistant to any rational conversation.

Rami took a resigned breath. "I teach things as they are. Nothing more. We should think progressively, but we are stuck in the past and the past has only given us grief. The only way we will be able to change the way we think is to change the way we think!"

"Who do you think you are? This is not the struggle we teach!" Assaf folded his arms doggedly.

"That is my case in point. You, sir, are a prime example of this stagnant thinking." Rami could feel his fury rising but kept his voice calm.

"Enough with your insults!" Assaf shouted." I will handle my son's education. And I will also speak to the other parents so that this nonsense will stop right here and now!" Still standing behind his father, Yasser winced.

"You are making a mistake!" Rami implored.

"My mistake was agreeing to let him go to your school!"

Rami turned to his brother for some help in the matter, but Marwan simply shrugged his shoulders in his usual, noncommittal way.

"What can I say to a man about his son's education?"

Rami was left holding out his hands as he watched Yasser being dragged away. He sat there stewing at the ignorance to which he'd just been subjected, when his brother put a hand on his shoulder.

"How is Lyda?" Marwan asked, his meaning intended as a reminder for Rami to pay more attention to his own family.

Rami answered with a quick brooding shrug of his shoulders.

Marwan remained undaunted. "My wife tells me she walks around the house ..."

"Like a ghost, I know...you told me!" There were days when Rami felt like everything was too much. This was one of them.

"Have you two been able to talk?" Marwan continued.

"What is there to talk about? What can I possibly... What is there to talk about?" Rami repeated. "There is this huge gaping hole between us that was once filled by our son."

Marwan let a respectful silence rest between them. Then asked, "Why don't you speak to that reporter? Maybe it would help?"

Rami looked at his brother skeptically. "Help who? Me? Her? You?" He looked around at the empty tables. "How is business these days anyway?" *Two can master the technique of non-sequiturs*, Rami thought.

Marwan sniffed and looked around. "Slow... as you can see. The security the IDF has built around us has killed everything."

"Yes, I never noticed until today that on weekdays I am often your only customer."

"Not true. Customers pay!" Marwan teased.

"You never let me pay," Rami countered.

"Of course not, you are my brother."

"Therefore, why would I pay?"

"Exactly."

"But when I come, it is with the intent of a customer." Rami added, to which Marwan had nothing. They both chuckled at the absurdity of the conversation.

The next day Rami waited impatiently at his desk in the classroom repeatedly checking his watch. "They should be here by now," he muttered to the empty room.

Restless he walked over to the window. Checking his watch again, he realized that Yasser's father had remained true to his word and had convinced the other parents to stop letting the boys come to class. Gathering up his things, he was about to head out when he heard a knock at the door. He looked up to see Christine Cooper standing in the doorway looking as determined as ever.

"Doctor Amar... Professor... is it a good time?" She asked.

"Actually, I was just leaving." Rami swung his jacket off the back of his chair.

Christine looked around the classroom. The smell of fresh paint still permeated the air. The notes on the blackboard were neatly organized, and the desks were arranged just so. "I just wanted to commend you on how well you've cleaned this place up."

"It seems all a waste of time now," Rami responded.

"Really? I heard it was going well."

"It was, I suppose, as well as it could have at least. But I should have understood that it was only a matter of time." Christine looked at him inquiringly. "It's the parents…" Rami continued. "They only think in one way, and it's very difficult to change people's minds around here. Hence…" He swung his arm to indicate the empty room.

They both stood in awkward silence until Christine finally offered, "When I was in school —it seems so long ago now —I used to tolerate the education part, you know, the Math, English, and History, because I was on the track team. I loved to run. I loved to compete —to strive to be better, faster. And I succeeded. I was a very good runner. Not anymore of course; but, at the time, that was how I was able to get a decent education… because of my athletic scholarship." They both fell into quiet thoughtfulness again until Christine added; "Maybe you can bribe them back with some soccer."

"Soccer balls are restricted here," Rami reminded her. "One was rigged with a bomb not long ago."

"Yes, I know, I covered it. But I'm sure an exception could be made for the right reasons. Anyway, what you're doing here..." Christine nodded at the room, "...is terrific! Why don't we talk about *this*?"

"There is no story here. Nothing worth talking about," Rami replied quickly.

Christine's brow furrowed. "Well, you're right about one thing; it *is* very difficult to change the way of thinking around here." She motioned to Rami, and he didn't disagree. She could see she was finally getting through to him and persisted. "You should let me determine what makes a good story. You know, I'm pretty good at what I do." Her confidence lit up her eyes.

Rami suddenly became lost in thought before he hurriedly re-gathered his things and rushed by Christine on his way out of the door.

"Ms. Cooper... the soccer thing. Thank you!" he said quickly, and then he was gone.

"Glad I could help," Christine mumbled as she wandered over to the blackboard for a closer look at his notes.

Rami continued his hurried pace until he reached his brother's café. Marwan was sitting at one of the tables reading a newspaper.

"Have you seen any of the kids this morning?" Rami rasped, out of breath.

Marwan just shook his head and turned the page.

"That is just wonderful! I was sitting up in the classroom all by myself... waiting! No one showed up!"

"Some kid in a wheelchair came around looking for you?"

"Oh? Who was he? What did he want?"

"I don't know, probably wants to join your class." Marwan closed his paper and motioned for Rami to come closer. His voice lowered. "I'm glad you came by, there was no one around to send for you. Imad will see you today at Aunt Suha's house at noon. Be discreet and be careful!"

Chapter 20

Rami leaned against the wall of a house glad to be in the shade. He wiped his brow with his handkerchief and checked his watch. It was noon. The air was stifling. Crossing the street, he entered through the small but heavy gate in the low wall of Aunt Suha's house, and walked cautiously through the tiny garden without disturbing so much as a stone.

Aunt Suha had passed away a few months earlier, and the house had remained empty since. It was bequeathed to her five children who were living in Dubai, Hong Kong, and New York. It had crossed Rami's mind to move in, but to reach all of her children and then get them to agree would be too long and difficult a process for which he had neither the energy nor the lack of dignity. Besides, he would be returning to Romania once things were settled, and Lyda would be better off staying with Marwan and Rose.

As Rami opened the front door, the sun brightened the otherwise dark interior. Stepping inside, he felt the cool relief wash over his body. At the far end of the house long white curtains billowed in and out of the window, dancing with the breeze created by the open door. He turned to close it behind him, and, as he did, the last brush of wind died, settling the curtains and revealing Imad.

Imad's hair was unkempt and he was several days unshaven. Rami thought his rogue appearance fit his mythical image well. "I have been trying to see you for weeks!"

The young man smiled confidently and respectfully at his uncle. "It's been too dangerous. They have been following you."

"They have?" Rami was shocked at the thought.

"Why else did they not throw you in jail for Hassan's actions?" Imad waited as Rami pondered the question. "Perhaps it was so you would lead them to me."

It made sense, thought Rami. He was not the only one who wanted to get to the bottom of his son's death; the Israelis were investigating also. What did that mean? Were there photographs of him teaching? Had someone been watching him with Lyda? He shivered. Had they been following him this whole time?

"Would you like something to drink?" Imad walked into the kitchen and opened the fridge door. "My father keeps the fridge stocked with overflow from the café."

Rami followed Imad but stopped at the kitchen entrance and looked around the room. He used to come here often as a young boy. His Aunt would make her delicious custard tart, and he would sit and eat the whole thing —the thin layer of biscuit, then the layer of chocolate, and then finally the top layer of vibrant yellow custard. He never lost the magic feeling of that dessert, or the image of Aunt Suha's smile as she watched him devour it all. He suddenly missed his favorite aunt, and the hole in his heart widened. "Tell me you had nothing to do with Hassan."

Imad closed the fridge door and looked into his uncle's eyes; "I am sorry about Hassan. He was my favorite cousin."

"Tell me!" Rami pressed.

"I had nothing to do with it!" Imad sat down at the small kitchen table and pulled out a chair.

Rami breathed a sigh of relief and walked over to join him. "What can you tell me about what happened to my son?"

"I know nothing," Imad replied.

"How is that possible? You know nothing." He waited for an answer that never came. "You know nothing?" He pressed a hand against his forehead as if trying to contain his anger.

"Understand that I am busy trying to stay alive, trying to keep my faction alive," Imad stated.

"There is a better way. There is still hope for you!"

Imad shook his head. "Do you realize how naive you sound? I am in too deep. I have done things that are unforgivable."

Rami was caught off guard by his nephew's remorseful tone and let his sympathy overpower him. "You could go away," he suggested.

"Like you?" The sudden acid in Imad's remark stung Rami to the core. "And then what?" Imad continued, "Leave this mess behind? It is easy for you to say. Only cowards walk away!"

Rami straightened. "Is that what you think I am?" It was time to have this conversation.

"It is what a lot of people think," Imad confirmed.

"Is that what *you* think?" Rami repeated. The two sat there in silence —the only sound the dripping of the tap in the kitchen sink.

"We needed you," Imad finally said.

"We? So, you *were* there that night!" Rami hissed. "You wanted me to contribute to the torture of another human being! How many finger nails did you finally peel off before you realized that poor boy didn't know anything —that you were wrong?" Rami's gaze bore into his nephew as he relived his rage. "I am a doctor trained to heal people. And you and your *cause* wanted my hands for something I was loath to do! And so now *I* am the coward?"

"We needed the intelligence. We thought he had it," Imad returned unapologetically.

"And then what? What were you going to do with it? You had no arms, no money, no organization!"

"We have come a long way since then, but you would know that had you stuck around!"

"I lost my only son to what? I don't even know. You... you are such a smart young man. You have everything it takes to have a better life, yet you chose to live like this."

Imad sighed. "I have heard this speech before from my father.

"He is right! You are constantly looking over your shoulder, always mistrusting. Even me... your own family!" Rami continued. "It's not too late, Imad! It's not too late!"

Imad stood up and leaned against the counter. ""It *is* too late. You have not been around. You don't know. You have no clue. And you have no respect for what I believe!"

"How and why am I supposed to respect what you believe when I have witnessed the things you have done?"

"I'd rather die fighting than live on my knees. That's why I do the things that you do not have the courage for," Imad said, his indignation hanging in the air like stale breath.

"That I do not have the *desire* for!" Rami spat back.

"You just don't get it! I would die for you!" Imad stepped closer to face his uncle.

Rami immediately stood to meet his eyes. "I don't want you to die for me! I want you to live for me!" A mixture of rage and sorrow surged through him.

"Lower your voice!" Imad insisted, his eyes shifting to the window. He was clearly concerned that their meeting might be detected.

After a moment, Rami's composure returned —his voice regaining its usual timbre. "Did you have anything to do with it?" He stared at Imad for any indication on his face, any sign of a lie. After a long silence, Rami asked again, more deliberately this time. "Did you have anything to do with it, Imad?"

Imad's brow furrowed and he looked away. "No. I did not need to encourage him; he was already there."

Rami closed his eyes as the truth sank in. "My family has lost too much blood, my blood, to your... *cause.*" He turned and paced around the kitchen, a tiger in a cage, until he stopped in front of his nephew. "I am teaching a group of boys up at the old school. They are good boys and I want to keep them that way. They have a future if they apply what I teach."

"Why are you telling me this?" Imad asked.

"Because I want you to stay away from them. Do not touch them. Leave them to another destiny, not the one you set for them; but the one I propose."

Imad shrugged his shoulders in Marwan's manner, as Rami continued to stare him down. Rami waited for a few seconds before heading for the door.

"And if I find out you had anything to do with Hassan's death… God help you!" *God help us all,* Rami thought. And, as he opened the front door to leave, the curtains billowed in the draft that crept through the old house.

Outside, the blaring sun offered respite from the abysmal conversation indoors. Rami's brow broke into a sweat almost immediately. He instinctively reached for his handkerchief; his attention drawn to some children playing by a small trickling of water spouting from a faucet in a wall. Despite his upset, he found himself marveling at how much joy a child could have just splashing about in water on a hot summer day. The sound of their laughter seemed pleasantly musical and calmed his nerves further. He squinted down the road and quickened his pace.

At the end of the street, he could hear what sounded like rolling thunder, which didn't make sense since there were no clouds in the sky. As the noise grew over the low-lying hills, he felt the rumble beneath his feet. Israeli gunships appeared overhead. They were nearly on top of him as the wind and dust swirled chaotically. Then, the sharp whistle of rockets pierced the air, quickly followed by an earth-shattering explosion.

Rami looked back at his aunt's house and saw a ball of smoke and flying debris erupt from within. He grabbed his head in horror and dropped to his knees as bits and pieces rained down all around him. "The children!" He cried. "The children!" As the helicopters turned and flew off, and the smoke cleared, his eyes landed on their small bodies writhing in the street. He spit the dust out from his mouth and ran to help.

Chapter 21

Inside his makeshift bunker office, Shani was on the phone when his attention was diverted by a commotion outside. As the argument grew louder, he recognized Rami's voice.

"I demand to see him right now!"

Corporal Cohen entered; his face flushed. "Sir, Dr. Amar insists on seeing you right away! I have searched him. He is clean."

Shani cupped the phone with his palm and nodded. "Let him in." He turned his attention back to the person on the other end of the receiver. "I'll have to call you back." Before he could hang up, Rami rushed in like a madman covered in dirt and bloodstains.

"You son of a bitch! You nearly killed a group of children… and me!"

"You look quite well to me," Shani replied.

"You used me so… so I could lead you to him; and then you murdered him!"

"There is no evidence of that!"

"Go look at the house! It's in ruins. The children were lying in the street bleeding."

"Thankfully there was a doctor nearby," Shani retorted. The sarcasm rolled off his tongue too easily, making him uncomfortable. "And watch your tone, or I will have you arrested and thrown in jail." Shani could feel his own anger rising up. He quelled it with a deep rasping sigh. "There is no evidence that anyone was killed."

Rami stared at him in disbelief. "But the house was demolished!"

"I've just received word that there were no bodies inside. Understand?"

Rami's head spun as he tried to absorb the Major's words.

"We missed him!" Shani admitted.

Relief washed over Rami and he tried to regain his composure. "I was trying to find out what happened to my son, and now..." He stopped, barely able to get the words past the bile in his throat, "... our children are bleeding in the street!" He paused to gauge any reaction from Shani but there was none. "It all makes me wonder who is worse, you or them!"

"Don't delude yourself Doctor! I do what I am told... what I have to do. Those are the rules. You must remember that there are always two sides to every tale."

A current of rage heated Rami's insides as he glared into what he now believed were the eyes of the devil. He spat defiantly on the floor in front of Shani who immediately bolted up, shoved his desk out of the way, and strode towards the doctor. Rami held his ground as they stood nose to nose. Corporal Cohen raced in; his weapon drawn.

"Get out!" Shani barked, but nobody moved. Shani turned his gaze to Cohen and pointed at him. "You! Out!!" Cohen retreated quickly; his face still flushed. Shani turned back to Rami. "You think you are the only one to lose somebody?" He pulled a small photo from his breast pocket and shoved it in Rami's face. "Do you know this man?" Before Rami could answer, Shani continued, "No, you don't! He was my best friend. My brother! We grew up together… played soccer together until the sun went down. I had not heard from him in years, and then he called me. I had just driven by him. He told me to turn around and come back to say hello." Shani shoved the picture back into his shirt pocket. "Then do you know what happened? Your son happened!"

Rami turned white and his legs weakened. He fell back into the chair behind him. Shani didn't budge. The memory infused him with loathing.

"I heard everything… every scream, every groan, every single last breath! When I arrived and saw him lying on the ground… the phone was still in his hand. In his hand!" Shani gritted teeth, "He was still on the line with me!"

"I had no idea. I don't know what to…" Rami was still in shock from the explosion, but now that was compounded by this sudden revelation.

Without warning, Shani quickly removed his sidearm and pressed it against Rami's forehead. "A thousand times I have pulled my gun out and blown your fucking brains out!"

Rami stared straight ahead strangely calm, ready for what might be his last moment alive, even if by accident.

"A thousand times I have wiped out your entire fucking village, every last one of you!" Shani paused; the doctor's eyes were calm but grief-stricken. Stepping back, Shani holstered his gun, leaving a red mark on Rami's forehead. He kicked his chair against the wall and began pacing like a caged animal, clearly conflicted by his own deep-rooted exasperation and his unexpected respect for the doctor. "Instead, I yell at my men; I smoke too much; and I grind my teeth when I sleep. When I sleep! It keeps my wife up at night!" A wry smile appeared on his face; "She says it's like sleeping with a growling tiger."

Rami saw the humor in his observation and detected the sweetness in which Shani related this intimacy.

"Like sleeping with a tiger," Shani repeated softly. He plunked down into his chair, closed his eyes, and massaged his temples with his thumb and forefinger. "So please, do not come in here as if you are the only victim." He opened his eyes and looked at Rami now as a peer. "We feel it too; every single time. And I am tired. I am exhausted!"

Rami stood up and approached him cautiously, but with all of the sincerity the moment required, "I am truly sorry for your loss."

Shani nodded. "I appreciate your condolences," he said, his voice as weary as his expression. "But our understanding of one another still doesn't change this whole fucking mess!"

Rami was at a loss for words. What could he say? The Major was correct. After a few minutes of silence, he slowly made his way to the door.

"Doctor! You should know that before you entered my office, I was talking to officials on the scene. The children were attended to and there were no serious injuries."

Rami turned around; "No *physical* injuries you mean. Who knows the trauma they will carry with them for the rest of their lives." Before exiting, he left one parting suggestion; "Your hand is bleeding, you should clean it. That old metal desk is probably rusty."

When the door closed, Shani looked down at his hand. Indeed, there was a trickle of blood on the edge of his palm, and he pulled out a handkerchief to stem it.

Chapter 22

Rami sat in Marwan's café dazed —his ears still ringing from the explosion. He contemplated the events of the last few hours. Questions bounced around in his brain. How could he be so foolish? Why would he *not* think they were tracking him? Of course, they were. Covert surveillance was standard protocol for the IDF. He leaned forward, cupping his hands over his ears to dull the ringing, feeling ashamed that he had led them to his nephew. He shook his head when he thought of how close he'd come to his own demise. He knew that they didn't care who else might have been in the house with Imad. Whoever it was would be guilty by association. *Another form of collective punishment*, Rami thought.

He felt betrayed but he could not make sense of why. Shani owed him nothing. They were no longer enemies, but they were certainly not friends. Now it made sense why the IDF had refrained from locking him up in jail —to keep an eye on his every move. And Lyda —what if they knew she had accepted money on behalf of Hassan? They would both be finished.

Rami mumbled under his breath, going over everything in his mind. He looked up to see Marwan leering at him from behind the counter. His brother was obviously resentful that he'd been talked into setting up the meeting in the first place.

"The meeting almost cost our son his life!" Marwan said, as if reading Rami's mind. Rami shook his head sorrowfully. Marwan's expression changed to one of concern. Grabbing a cola from the fridge, he wandered around the counter to his brother's table. "But I don't blame you. These Israeli's are ruthless and clever and will stop at nothing to destroy us all." Regardless of his anger, Marwan would always be Rami's protector. He never could stand seeing his little brother hurt. He slid the cola across the table, his eyes full of compassion.

Rami cupped the bottle in his hands and nodded to his brother gratefully. As Marwan turned to attend to another customer, Rami heard a shuffling noise at the entrance of the café. He looked over to see a young boy of about fourteen, unsuccessfully trying to maneuver his wheelchair over the lip of the entrance. Rami leapt up to help. "Here, let me!" He took the handles of the chair, tipped up the front wheels, and pushed the boy inside.

"Thank you!" The boy struggled to push the wheels through the maze of chairs but gave up. He was slight and pale with reddish hair and grey eyes that appeared weighted by sadness. "You are Doctor Amar, Hassan's father?"

'I am," Rami replied.

"I have been looking for you. My name is Omar. Hassan died because of me!"

Rami was taken aback. Unsure of how to react, he steered the wheelchair to his table, pushing a chair out of the way to make room, and sat opposite the boy.

"I was released from the hospital yesterday. Your son was my best friend. The best, best friend anyone could ever have."

Rami looked intensely at Omar, trying to ascertain what was coming next, when he realized Marwan was standing over him with another soda in his hands. Marwan placed it down without a word, and left them to their conversation.

As Rami and Omar sat sipping their sodas, Omar began.

"Hassan and I were walking to the Town Square talking about what new CD's our music man would be selling that day, when I noticed our man in his usual spot near the fountain..."

"There he is!" Omar pointed, barely able to contain himself. Hassan looked over to see 'The Music Man' —a teenager a few years older than both of them, sitting on a milk crate in front of other crates, holding bootleg CD's.

"Ok, let me go get some smaller bills first so that I can bargain with him," Hassan said, turning in the direction of the newsstand.

Omar was too excited to wait. "I'm going over to see what he's got!"

"Ok then; I'll just be a few minutes. Omar, don't make any deals until I get there!"

At the far end of an intersecting street, an Israeli military vehicle pulled up. Several soldiers disembarked and took up positions, training their scopes on the opposite end of the town's square. A youth rally in near full frenzy emerged, moving in the soldiers' direction. Forty or more young men and boys marched and chanted in angry protest as they waved flags and posters of dead family members.

Hassan entered the newsstand. A bell jingled his arrival alerting a wily old man behind the counter who looked up from his newspaper. The fragrant aroma of Turkish coffee permeated the air, as Hassan walked towards him.

"Can you break this for me please?" He asked, holding up a bill.

"I cannot. I have barely sold anything today." The owner was an old hand at negotiation and knew better than to just break someone's money without profiting from it. "Perhaps you should buy something, that way I will have to give back some change."

Hassan smiled, knowing the game all too well. He looked around and picked up the least expensive pack of gum he could find. The old man laughed at his acumen, but a deal was a deal.

Outside, the demonstration had already reached the fountain. The marchers began shouting at the soldiers and hurling stones. Omar and the Music Man were confused, unsure of what to do. Suddenly, shots rang out and the mob panicked, scattering in all directions. Omar froze, caught in a hail of bullets.

Inside the store, Hassan and the old man were startled by the sound of gunfire. Hassan ran to the window to see Omar pinned against the low wall of the fountain, bullets spitting up around him, pockmarking the ground and wall. Dropping the gum, he charged for the door, the old man shouting after him.

"Don't go out there! Are you crazy?"

Hassan ignored him and bolted outside, hugging the wall as he made his way toward his terrified friend.

Omar lay writhing in pain as blood pooled around his legs, filling the small craters in the old cement. The shooting ceased as quickly as it had begun, but the soldiers remained in position. The protesters had backed off down the road several meters away, but remained defiant. In the aftermath, two other bodies lay in the street either already dead or very nearly.

Hassan made a desperate dash across the road to his friend's side. Tears streamed down Omar's cheeks as he screamed in terror.

"Hold on! Hold on! Where are you hit?" Hassan asked frantically.

Shaking uncontrollably, Omar could barely speak. "I don't know, I can't feel anything! I can't feel!"

Hassan looked around and spotted an idling car that had been abandoned during the gunfire. He ran over and jumped in, jamming it into gear and steering it as close as he could to his friend. Jumping back out, he dragged Omar to the car using all his might to get him into the back seat.

As he tore through the streets, Hassan could only think of one hospital nearby, but he would have to go through a roadblock and that would be a problem. As the car bounced and swerved through the rough, dirt roads, Omar drifted in and out of consciousness. In the fleeting moments he was awake, he mumbled something about bleeding all over someone's nice back seat and how upset they would be with him when they found out.

Hassan finally came to a screeching halt outside the cement barriers of the first checkpoint where several rifles were trained on the car. "I must get to a hospital right away! Please let me through!" He screamed.

"This checkpoint is closed! No one is to come in or out!" A soldier yelled back.

"He is dying! I must get him to a doctor!"

"I already told you this checkpoint is closed!"

"Look! Look at him in the back seat! He is bleeding to death!" Hassan was hysterical now. He could see the soldier was conflicted as he cautiously moved in for a closer look. When the soldier saw the blood everywhere he recoiled slightly but remained steadfast.

"I'm sorry, but I have my orders!"

"Then I am driving through right now!"

"Then you will be shot… right now!" The soldier leveled his gun.

Hassan was enraged. He slammed the car into reverse and made a violent one-hundred-and-eighty degree turn. As he accelerated away, he screamed one last insult out his window. "You are all sons of whores!"

Hassan drove from one checkpoint to another, but none of the soldiers would let him through because of the incident in the town's square. By the time he reached the final checkpoint, both the car and its passengers were running on fumes. Hassan stepped out of the car and looked around pleadingly as soldiers stared at him through their rifle sights. He looked into the back seat. His friend was motionless, maybe dead.

Helpless and at a complete loss, Hassan covered his face and dropped to his knees trying to hold back his tears. His heart raced and his breath was erupting through his chest. "Father! Where are you? Where are you?" He cried, his heartbreaking wail echoing through the barren countryside.

As the dirt dug into his knees and the soldiers looked on, Hassan's mind drifted to other sons who had called out to fathers who could not protect them. He slowly stood up, and, as if in a trance, walked away. He walked away from the checkpoint, the soldiers, and his friend dying in the back seat of a car. He walked away from his hopes and dreams, away from an education, away from a career in medicine like his father, and away from the prospect of falling in love and having a family. His mind was made up. He walked away from it all…

Chapter 23

In the café, Rami looked away remorsefully, ashamed at his absence. A thick knot sat at the base of his throat as Hassan's cry for him echoed throughout his body.

"I was in and out of consciousness, but I do remember waking up inside a military vehicle, and hearing the voices in Hebrew that were attending me." Omar looked down when he finished, the sadness creeping back into his eyes. It was obvious that survivor's guilt still enveloped him.

Rami had sat engrossed by Omar's recollection, realizing how difficult it was for him to tell his story. He admired the boy's mettle and felt a surge of warmth for Hassan's loyal and caring friend.

"I wouldn't be alive today…" Omar indicated to the wheelchair he sat in, "…if Hassan hadn't taken me to the checkpoints, and the Israelis hadn't intervened."

Rami took a deep breath. A sense of relief in knowing what had motivated Hassan flowed through him like a sugar rush. And then, once again, the grief that was ever present returned.

"All I know is that Hassan saved my life! He did everything in his power to get me the help I needed." Omar removed a letter from his pocket and unfolded it. "He sent me this letter while I was in the Israeli hospital, just before he…" He paused finally realizing how hard this must have been for Rami. "He did it because of what happened to me." Omar leaned forward and read the opening lines…

"Because I am so fed up with the oppression and the lack of compassion in the face of our circumstances. And, because I cannot take being this helpless anymore; this… insignificant.!"

"I'm sorry, I can't read it again. It hurts too much," Omar said as he handed the letter over to Rami. The paper was crisp and clean, the penmanship elegant. Rami remembered the hours

Lyda had spent teaching Hassan how to write. His body shrank under the weight of the air surrounding him. He looked down at the letter in his hand but could not read it. He needed time.

"I tell you he was the best friend anyone could ever have," Omar repeated.

Rami agreed with a nod and a rueful smile as he reached out to hold the boy's hand.

Later that evening, Rami stood at the open door to the bedroom and watched Lyda as she stood by the window. The curtains on either side of her danced gracefully in the gentle evening breeze, and the light of the moon created a soft halo around her lithe figure. Rami came up behind her, gently took her hand, and drew her to the bed. They sat together in silence for a while, breathing in the herbs from Rose's small garden.

"I met a young boy today… a friend of Hassan," Rami began.

When he had finished, Lyda had her face in her hands. She was crying —as moved by Omar's story as her husband. Rami knelt in front of her, not unlike the day he had proposed, and gently took her hands away from her face.

She looked at him, tears streaming down her cheeks. "I would like to meet this boy," she whispered.

He put a hand on her knee and she placed her hand over his. Looking deeply into her sweet brown eyes, he smiled and nodded —his heart warmed by this private moment between them. Such intimacy bound them together even more, cementing their journey towards healing.

Chapter 24

Standing in the empty classroom, Rami stared out of the window and thought long and hard about what he could do of significance in such a place. He jotted his ideas down on a notepad, and then looked across the field at the boulder. It rested like some meteor that had landed a million years ago and now lay fixed in time.

He returned his pen and notepad to his bag and made his way back down to the village, his eyes resting on the fountain square. He had already arranged to meet the boys there. He hoped they would show up.

Sitting down on the edge of the fountain, he squinted at the bright light of midday and dropped his bag at his feet. He looked around, his thoughts replaying Omar's story again and again. He heard the rally, the gunfire, the screams, and the last whispered breaths of those who fell. He looked at the parched earth and saw the bullet holes and bits of debris still scattered around. No one had bothered to clean up after that fateful day. He dug his heel into one of the holes and thought of the damage the bullet that made it could do to a body. The fountain's water ran behind him and circulated in a constant gentle flow.

A group of boys rounded the corner and walked towards him. Rami pulled out his handkerchief to wipe his brow as he stood up. Rafik, Yasser, and a few other classmates hovered around him, while others sat down on the wall.

"Thank you all for coming. I will get right to the point," Rami said, pocketing his handkerchief. "I will make you a deal that you will all find irresistible." He couldn't understand why he was feeling so nervous. "For every day you come to school, we will play one hour of football at the end of it."

The boys stood waiting for more, but that was it. As always, Rafik spoke first. "So… you want us to play football every day?"

"Actually, I want you to go to school every day, and then we play football *after* school," Rami replied.

Rafik thought for a moment, his eyes suspicious. "But how can we play with the rock in the middle of the field?" There was a chorus of agreement.

"We will play around it."

"What do you mean "around it"?" Yasser asked

"I admit it seems strange but think of it as a new rule… a challenge!" Rami felt he was reaching. This was harder than he'd anticipated.

"But how are we supposed to play with a big boulder in the middle of the field?" Rafik repeated, obviously unsatisfied.

"Don't worry, I'll get rid of it!" Rami had no idea how he would accomplish such a feat, but the words had left his mouth before he could stop himself. Judging by the looks on their faces, no one believed him. "I will be your coach," Rami added, but this excited the boys even less.

"I can play anywhere, anytime, and I don't need to go to school every day to do it." Rafik folded his arms together defiantly.

"Yes…" said Rami reaching into his bag, "…but you cannot play with this!" He held up a shiny new soccer ball, the fresh black and white leather popping in the sunlight.

The boys' eyes grew wide and their mouths fell open. A barrage of "Wows!" followed. Like lost souls walking towards the light, their attention had been directed to the prize. The ball was the cherry that made Rami's deal tantalizing. Sure, they could play anywhere, any time, but they would be kicking around an old milk jug, or rolled up newspapers and twine —some cheap, destructible imitation of the real thing.

Everyone knew that soccer balls had been banned in their region. Ever since a bomb, hidden inside a ball, was rolled into a crowd and detonated, the IDF had outlawed them. Anyone caught with one — even a child —could be locked up. Since this particular ball came from the Israeli's, and was cleared by Major Shani himself, it was assured there would be no repercussions.

At first, Shani had put up his usual resistance; but when Rami assured him that the ball would always remain in his possession, the Major could find no valid reason why a soccer ball should be refused. "It will only be used at the school, and if it ever disappears you will report it immediately!"

Rami knew that the enthusiasm of the boys would work wonders on their skeptical parents. Soccer had powers of persuasion that nothing else could match. He was certain the boys would show up.

The next day, Rami was preparing his lessons at his desk when he heard a familiar shuffling at the door. He looked up to see Omar struggling to maneuver his wheelchair through the doorway with a little help from a girl close to his age.

"Zara, let go!" The girl stood back, her expression annoyed as Omar backed up the wheelchair and tried entering again, sweat glistening on his forehead.

Rami stood up. "What a pleasant surprise! But, can't we help you?"

Omar waved him off determined to do it on his own. "What good is an assistant coach if he always needs to be assisted?" Omar quipped, as he finally pushed himself through.

"Assistant coach?" Rami smiled, admiring the temerity of the boy. "Well… I suppose you are correct. Please find a place that is comfortable for you." He stepped out of the way as he acknowledged the young girl who remained standing in the doorway.

"This is my cousin," said Omar. "She helped me up the hill."

Rami smiled at Zara who sullenly looked away under his gaze. She was a tall girl with long legs and a faint scar under her right eye.

"I'll come back later to help you back down," she said curtly to Omar before quickly leaving.

As they waited for the rest of the class to show up, Omar shared with Rami how life had changed for him since returning home — how his family had been coping with the new challenges his wheelchair posed; how the neighbors had donated wood for a ramp so that he could access the front door of his house; and how his mother exercised his legs every day and rubbed homemade ointment into his scars believing it would heal them. "Plus, my wheelchair was donated by the Israeli hospital where the staff took care of me," he continued. "It's ironic to think that the Israelis also donated the bullet that caused all of this." He smiled sadly. "I don't hate them, you know. We've hurt their children too."

Rami nodded. Being confronted by his mortality appeared to instill in Omar even more compassion than Rami himself possessed. He looked at the boy's thick lashes and bright, intelligent eyes with the thought that this music-loving teenager was a great role model for others.

When the rest of the boys finally showed up, Rami reminded them that he expected them all to be prompt. "Anyone who is late without a valid reason will be scratched from that day's game," he warned. "But since this is your first day back, today is not included."

He walked to the blackboard and chalked up the first question of the day. When he turned back to the class, a flock of hands excitedly shot into the air, voices garbled, as everyone spoke out simultaneously.

'Whoa, whoa, one at a time! Yes, Yasser!" Rami pointed, surprised to see him there.

"When do we play?" Yasser asked followed by a chorus of agreement from the class.

"After classes… always after classes. I am no fool. Do you think I will get you back in here after soccer?" Rami smiled. The boys looked at each other, not pleased with the answer. Still, with a collective shrug of their shoulders, they acquiesced.

"Okay, so get out your notebooks — I hope you brought them — and write down the question on the board."

There was a rustling of paper as everyone did as they were told. Rami began pacing back and forth in front of his desk, waiting. He stopped short when Lyda suddenly appeared at the doorway. She looked at him with an uneasy smile and marched forward carrying a basket in her hand, a few girls trailing behind her.

"I apologize for interrupting," she said, as much to Rami as to the rest of the class. "I brought lunch in case no one thought that school and soccer might make everyone hungry."

Rami smiled, took the basket from her, and placed it on his desk. "Class, this is my wife, Lyda," he said, as she smiled at his students.

"And this is Nayla and Fatima, and this angel I found hanging around outside is Zara," Lyda returned. "They would like to join the class." The girls stepped forward, as the boys grumbled amongst themselves. Omar looked at Zara and was about to say something, but thought otherwise.

Yasser stood up and pulled a chair over to an empty desk beside him. "You can sit here, Fatima," he said smiling awkwardly. The rest of the boys laughed, and Yasser's ears turned pink.

"There are more girls who would like to join," Lyda continued as she directed the girls to sit. "School is for everyone."

Rami smiled broadly and nodded. "Of course, it is. We would be happy to fill the classroom with whomever is interested."

Rafik's hand shot up into the air. "But they're not playing soccer with us, right?"

"I can play better than you!" Zara glared at Rafik. Her long dark hair was pulled back into a tight ponytail, and she looked quite capable of defending herself if necessary. Rafik's hand returned to his desk.

Lyda smiled again and this time the whole class smiled back. She noticed Omar off to the side in his wheelchair and approached him. Leaning in, she held her hand to her heart. "You must be Omar! I've heard wonderful things about you." The shy boy blushed and placed his hand on his heart in greeting her.

Behind them, Rami peeked into the basket hoping that his wife's cooking had improved. Unlike her delicious coffee, her meals were either too dry, too over-seasoned, or too bland. But everything looked surprisingly good. *Besides, the children won't care*, he thought. *Food is food.*

He watched Lyda's easy way with his pupils. She was so loving and nurturing towards them, and they responded to her immediately. "Class, why don't we all thank *Aunt Lyda* for her thoughtful gesture of lunch today?"

The various appreciations echoed through the room with Lyda playfully brushing them off. "Well, I should go so you can continue to educate these young minds," she said as she turned back to Rami. He held out his hand and she took it momentarily as she walked by him. Rami's heart swelled as he looked into her eyes. There was an easy way about her now —an obvious physical transformation, brought on by her decision to contribute to the school. Her skin was clear and glowing, and her expression calm. As she waved goodbye to the class, he felt himself falling in love with her all over again.

As soon as Lyda left, Yasser's hand was up, waving urgently.

Rami sighed. "Yes Yasser. What is your question?"

"When do we eat?"

The whole class laughed —everyone nodding in solidarity.

Rami just shook his head in resignation and put down his chalk. "Fine! Yasser you will be our taste tester!" He picked up the basket and began removing the carefully wrapped and rolled pita sandwiches. He handed one to Yasser. "Here you go. Tell us what that tastes like!"

Yasser took a bite, chewed for a minute, and then smiled. Rami was intrigued and tried one for himself. The sandwich was delicious. No doubt Lyda had been taking lessons from Rose who was a notoriously good cook. He smiled, and then with the aid of Yasser and Rafik he began handing out sandwiches to the rest of the class.

Later that day when Rami arrived at Marwan's house, he went straight to the bedroom deep in thought. He sat absent-mindedly on the edge of the bed and looked around. His suitcase was sitting upright on the floor near the window. He retrieved it, plopped it on the bed, and opened it, studying its contents. Then, he unpacked slowly, placing his clothes in the bureau, hanging up his jackets, and carefully placing Hassan's letters in a drawer. Once he was done, he replaced the empty case in the back of the closet where Lyda had originally put it. And that was that. He had decided he wouldn't be going anywhere for quite some time. He would begin rebuilding his life here, and it would start with the love of his life. Now that the IDF was watching him, the chances of him being called on in the middle of the night had greatly diminished. He and Lyda were safe for now.

Chapter 25

The next day's class went very well. As a result, the football game afterwards was played with exulted energy. The ball took flight from a sharp kick and landed among a scurry of feet that kicked up dust all around in an attempt to gain control. Rami and Omar watched from the sidelines coaching and cheering everyone on.

Rafik, the best player among them, took over the ball and attempted a cross-field pass. The ball curved and bounced off the boulder, sending it in the opposite direction of his intended path. Zara caught the ball with her foot and passed it to Fatima who, in a breakaway, headed towards the makeshift goal. She darted to the left and then kicked to the right. The goalie leaped up to catch it but missed —the ball ending up in the corner of the net. Fatima fell on her knees in triumph, the rest of her team racing over, patting her on the back, and cheering.

Rafik shook his head in disbelief. "This is ridiculous! How can you play a proper game with this hellish rock in the middle of the field?" He stomped away; his frustration obvious with every step. "How can a *man* play a proper game?" He headed down the path towards the village.

"Rafik, come back! The game's not over!" Rami shouted.

"It is for me! You wanted me to try it; I did. I told you we couldn't play here!"

"Rafik, don't go!" Yasser pleaded.

"You said you would get rid of that stupid rock!" Rafik challenged. "I am finished with this game, with this field, and with this god-forsaken school!" The other boys looked at each other and then, one by one followed him. The girls looked at each other, shrugged, and followed soon after.

Rami was disheartened. The boys would not want to continue without their best player on the field and their loyalties were to him. Just when he thought he had them all back, he'd lost them once again.

With nothing left to do, he headed back to the café where Christine was waiting for him, her van parked nearby. Marwan brought each of them coffee and then left them alone to talk.

Rami was clearly agitated. "What do you want me to say? I don't want to be interviewed. I don't want my pain to be splattered all over the newspapers and airwaves!"

Christine nodded sympathetically. "I know this is hard. I do, believe me. But I think it's important to tell your family's point of view; to talk about the fallout; to let others know how you and your wife are dealing with it all."

"How we are dealing with it?" Rami bore into her. "How do you deal with it?"

Christine stiffened, clearly struck by her own loss.

"No, tell me! How did you feel, Ms. Cooper? Numb? Do you walk around like a ghost? Are you so lost in your grief you cannot breathe at times? Does your mind ever release you from it?"

Christine hung her head. "I still wake up every day filled with dread, hoping it's all just a nightmare." She looked up, her eyes tearing. "There is nothing worse than this kind of heartache." There was a long pause between them.

"Add to that that our child was responsible for other deaths." Rami continued. "It becomes more than heartache. It becomes unspeakable."

"I wish you were more familiar with my work," Christine said, with a tinge of hope in her voice. "There is an important story here, Dr. Amar — a story that turned grief into action. Maybe we can talk about what you're doing with the school and the kids. It's so positive, and yet, isn't it a reaction, or a result, of what happened to Hassan?"

Rami twisted the napkin in his hands. "I don't know how much difference it's making. It's a struggle every day just to get these kids to show up."

"But at least *someone* around here is trying to make a difference," Christine added.

She was tenacious; Rami would give her that. "I am not ready to talk to anyone about anything yet."

His eyes drifted away as he dropped his napkin onto the table.

Christine backed off. "Well, I am sorry to hear that, but I *do* understand." She stood up. "You did say *yet*, so perhaps one day?" She held out her hand.

Rami accepted her handshake. "Perhaps." He watched her leave, his mind returning to the day's events and Rafik's influence on the other children. *Perhaps not*, he thought to himself.

Chapter 26

The following morning, Rami sat at his school desk waiting impatiently, hoping that what he feared was not true. He looked over at Omar and Zara who had pencils and papers ready —the only two students who'd shown up thus far. Rami forced a smile, looked at his watch again and shook his head. This was not good. He wandered over to the window and looked out to see if anyone was coming up the hill but didn't see a soul. He returned to the blackboard and grabbed a piece of chalk.

"Okay, let's get started."

As he began writing, he heard a low rumble in the distance. Omar and Zara rushed to the window. Dropping the chalk, he joined them to see a cloud of smoke rising on the far side of the village. Fear seized his heart.

"What is it?' Omar asked.

"I don't know." Rami looked at Omar and Zara's concerned faces, memories of his recent ordeal at his aunt's house sending an involuntarily quiver throughout his body. "I've got to go," he added quickly. "Will you two be okay here by yourselves?"

"Yes, we'll be fine… go, go!"

Rami swiped his jacket off the back of the chair and raced out.

By the time he arrived, a crowd of cursing and wailing men and women had gathered at the scene. As Rami made his way through them, he saw the faces of his traumatized students looking on in horror and disbelief. On the ground, near a small, blackened crater, the remains of Yasser lay covered in blood. It took a moment for the image to sink in, but as soon as Rami realized who he was looking at, he recoiled. Everything below Yasser's torso was gone. A medic snapped a white sheet into the air, which floated like a cloud above the small boy until it landed softly over his body.

Rami quickly scanned his students and realized that many of them were not only still in shock, but also partially deaf from the concussive effect of the explosion. Their eyes were drawn towards Yasser's torn body as if a powerful magnet was forcing their gaze and they could not pull away —an image they could not un-see — a trauma they would never fully recover from.

Spotting Rafik amongst the crowd, Rami made his way to his side and put a hand on his shoulder, drawing his attention away from the gruesome site. As their eyes met, he knew that the boy before him had changed forever.

"A bunch of us stole some cigarettes, and we were looking for a place to sit and smoke," Rafik admitted, his whole body shaking. Rami took off his jacket and gently placed it around Rafik's thin shoulders. "Yasser was ahead of us when he saw something shiny in the ground. He ran over and nudged it with his foot."

The explosion had been abrupt with Yasser disappearing in a curtain of fire and earth, as the horrified boys looked on. They could not comprehend what they had witnessed. Yasser had called to them first; then, he had simply vanished amid the deafening blast — blood splattering. Rafik was the first to run towards what was left of his friend.-Now, he pulled Rami's jacket tight to his chest, brow creased, reliving the moment as his mind roiled. His distraught mother pushed her way through the crowd. Rushing over, she embraced him tightly, tears of relief staining her tanned cheeks. When she was certain her son was unharmed, she turned to face Rami.

"Everyone knows there's military debris scattered in the overgrowth on this side," she cried, her eyes full of bitterness. "I don't know why our children don't listen to us. Do they think they're invincible?" Rami shook his head sympathetically, and watched after her as she maneuvered her way back through the crowd, Rafik held tightly by her side.

Looking around as the crowd thickened, Rami noticed Christine and Greg near the blast preparing to cover the incident. Christine tepidly inched closer to get a better look inside the crater, and then instantly turned and walked away, the microphone dangling at her side. Rami knew this was not a normal reaction for a professional accustomed to seeing such things on a regular basis. Christine's shoulders were folded inward, her chin to her chest as her legs shifted beneath her, directionless. Making his way over, he put a gentle hand on her shoulder and she turned to him with tears in her eyes.

"I need to call my boss," she said quietly, her face pale and drawn.

"Wait," he replied. "Take a few minutes to calm your thoughts and breathe. Then call him."

"Yes, of course." Christine inhaled slowly. After a minute or so, she pulled out her phone. "I'm better now," she said, nodding at Rami. "Really."

Rami watched as she drifted away from him; she was unlike other reporters he'd met over the years. She appeared *invested* in the area. If he ever did decide to share his story then she would be the one to interview him. As he pondered this sudden revelation, Greg stepped up beside him, cradling his camera on his hip.

"She'll be alright," he offered looking at his colleague as she held the phone to her ear. "She's just... it's been a rough year for her."

"Yes," Rami concurred. "I believe she's tougher than she looks." He nodded at Greg and then focused his attention back to the boys. *However, not all of us have her resiliency,* he thought, as he walked back into the crowd to help wherever he could.

Chapter 27

Rami was distraught as he sat at the kitchen table in his brother's house. Marwan was brewing tea, and peered over at him periodically. Rami could see that his brother also felt the weight of Yasser's unexpected death, but he could offer him no solace. His mind was spinning, and his thoughts came spurting out in a rambling tirade.

"I had him in my hands. I had him! He was there… coming every day. They were all coming, and then they just stopped! All because of that god forsaken boulder in the middle of the field! Imagine that! A damned rock! A rock in the middle of that damned football field! If only…"

"This is hard for all of us," Marwan interrupted, as he brought the piping hot teapot over and set it on the table. "Please try to calm yourself." But Rami couldn't, his anger was rising and his mind was in full sprint. He pounded his fists on the table bouncing the teapot and sputtering the scalding liquid everywhere.

"An albatross around my neck —around everyone's neck, that's what it is! I will get rid of it! I *must* get rid of it!" he declared, more to himself than Marwan.

"Rami, relax! There is nothing you could have done. It was a terrible accident." Marwan wiped off the table, obviously annoyed

"Where can I get some explosives?"

"What?"

"Explosives!" Where can I get some? I want to blow that dammed thing sky high!" Rami jumped up and began moving around the room like a downed, live, electrical wire. "Where can I get some explosives?" He asked again.

"Lower your voice! You are speaking like a madman!" Marwan looked around, making certain no one had heard anything.

"Where?" Rami insisted.

"Stop it! You are not going to get any explosives, and certainly not for a rock! Come back to earth, brother! Anybody I know would never part with those types of munitions; they're too valuable. Besides, you would be labeled a terrorist if you were caught with them. Don't you see? There would be an immediate investigation into the materials used, where they came from, and how that stuff found its way into your possession!"

Rami knew that Marwan was right, but couldn't stop himself. "What about your son?"

"What about him? He would be the first one to tell you to go screw yourself!"

"Well then, how else can I get rid of the boulder?"

"Forget about the god forsaken boulder!"

Rami looked at his brother and realized quickly that his patience had gone.

"There is no need to raise your voice!"

"Yes, there is! You make me crazy!" Marwan slammed the cups down on the table and began pouring. "Now have some god forsaken tea and relax!"

Marwan's thundering voice clashed with the gentle pouring of the tea, sobering Rami's mania.

"I'll relax when you stop yelling!" Rami demurred as he gently picked up the steaming cup.

Marwan shook his head, exasperated, and eased himself into the chair opposite his brother. They both remained there for a while, each in their own thoughts, sipping their tea in silence.

Chapter 28

Early next morning, Rami headed to the school before anyone else in the household was up. He stood staring at the boulder for a while before trying everything he could think of, to remove it on his own.

He began by tying one end of sturdy rope around its circumference, and the other end to Marwan's donkey, but the effort proved futile. He spoke to a local farmer and added two more horses to the rope, but still, the object would not budge. Then, he talked the same farmer into bringing his tractor to the field offering to pay for the fuel. The tractor ended up in a standstill, and the farmer gave up, insisting Rami also pay for any damages incurred.

Rami had become obsessed, yet everything he continued to try, failed. The rock was as unmoving as the mountain it came from. There was only one other option he could think of that was sure to get the job done.

The following day, Rami sat across from Shani in his small checkpoint office. Shani stared back at him for a long moment not quite sure he'd heard correctly. After his usual pursed lips and heavy exhale, he scratched his head. "You are a very odd man!"

"Flattery will not get rid of my boulder," Rami countered.

"You are serious?" Shani was incredulous.

"Absolutely!"

"Why do you waste my time with this? You come here with these outrageous requests as if I owe you something!"

"It was your shelling that knocked it loose from the hills in the first place! You put it there. You get rid of it!" Rami replied.

"Why don't you ask one of your relatives? Surely one of them is cooking up some explosives somewhere nearby?"

Rami smiled; Israeli's were known for their darkly skewed, pragmatic sense of humor, and Shani was no exception. "I have no knowledge of any such activity... and believe me, don't think I haven't tried!" he relayed back.

Shani looked at him for a long, contemplative moment. "Please get out of my office. I don't have time for this nonsense!"

"This is not nonsense! What is nonsense is that there are boys who I could have in my class every day, but instead they are outside kicking around live ammunition that your troops leave behind. You are killing our children and..."

"Watch what you are saying!" Shani's eyes bore into Rami.

Cohen poked his head in the door. "Everything alright?" A quick glare from Shani and he retreated back to his post.

Shani studied Rami's face. "There is a cease fire right now and peace negotiations are about to commence… again. How will it look if we point our gunships at a schoolyard?"

"It is for a just cause." Rami replied, his expression determined.

Shani knew that, as usual, he would not get rid of Rami so easily. After a brief moment he sighed. "You are worse than my own children when they want something."

Rami looked at the photograph, face down on the Major's desk. He instinctively reached for it but Shani flinched, which stopped him. Then, changing his mind, Shani turned the picture upright so that Rami could see it for the first time. He looked at it and smiled. "You have a lovely family. The young one has a real sense of humor —you can see it in her eyes."

Shani looked at the photo and realized that the doctor was correct — not that he hadn't noticed the humor in Hofit's eyes before, but rather that he'd taken it for granted and hadn't noticed it in the picture. "She rules the house," he said, with a smile only a proud father could emit. He turned the picture to face him and reached for his phone. "Would you step out for a moment while I make a call?"

"Thank you!" Rami stood to leave, satisfied that Shani would at least make an effort.

Once Rami was completely outside, Shani placed the phone back on the cradle as he thought for a moment about how best to approach the topic with his superiors. Then, he picked up the handle again and began dialing.

Rami stepped out from the dark, cool bunker into the bright sunlight, and squinted as his eyes adjusted. The young soldiers on guard were beginning to get used to him. One of them drew out a cigarette, lit it, and then looked up to see Rami staring at him. He held out the pack, but Rami shook his head.

Stepping away from the soldiers, he walked into the middle of the road. He looked up and down the deserted stretch and recalled growing up nearby — how, as children, he, Marwan, and Marwan's friends would walk around for miles looking for anything to occupy their time. If they came across snakes, Marwan and his friends would kill them because... they were snakes. Turtles would get crushed with large rocks because they ate the greenery the farmers attempted to grow. Rami was a pacifist —a lover of all life —and had protested wildly in an attempt to save the creatures; but he was always outnumbered, so the killings continued.

Walking to the edge of the road, he studied the hills surrounding the bunker. If he hadn't set his mind on becoming a doctor, he could have easily become an archeologist. He remembered back to the day he and Marwan were exploring, and discovered a cave with an old urn buried halfway under the sand. This particular clay pot had piqued his interest because of the rudimentary design etched into it, obviously while the clay was still soft and malleable. The depiction would remain burned into his mind always —a man, a sun, and squiggly waves of water.

When Rami brought it home and showed his father, it was suggested they take it to a local to have it authenticated. The man they brought it to told them to leave it with him for a few days. Rami never saw the urn again. Rami shook his head remembering the audacity of the man and how he had claimed the urn was stolen from his shop. Most likely, he had realized the artifact's value, and sold it to an Israeli museum.

A few soldiers drifted towards Rami, and he turned to greet them. He looked at their young faces and noted that they appeared as fed up with the situation in the West Bank as everyone else. "Did you know that some of the oldest artifacts, which sit in your museums, came from this region?" he informed them. The soldiers looked at each other wondering which one of them actually knew that. None of them, it appeared. Rami went on. "It is true! Sold by our people to your people, probably for a song, a meal for the day, or a horse."

Rami was still lecturing when Shani emerged from his office and walked out to the middle of the road where all of his soldiers had gathered. "Well Doctor, that was an interesting discussion," he said, as he led Rami back to the bunker. He had just put down the phone with Colonel Moss who'd been relaxing at home watching a soccer game, so he'd caught him in a good mood. "I have spoken with my superior, who is also a friend of mine. He says *if* he can make this happen —this unusual request of yours —there will be conditions. Well... one specific condition."

Rami was caught off guard. "Well... yes... I imagine there would have to be."

"He's suggested a game. He wants your team to play his son's team from the settlement. They have no one to play with but themselves, and they have grown tired of that."

Rami thought about it for a moment, intrigued by the proposal. "I would have to ask the children first, of course."

"I should think it would be a great opportunity for them to show off their skills!" Shani smiled.

"But what about security?"

"The area is already sealed off now, so we will take care of any additional measures. And, perhaps you can talk to your brother, seeing that he knows so many people —make sure there are no incidents from your side.

Rami warmed quickly to the idea, as his growing smile attested. He thanked the Major and began walking away. "You get rid of that rock and I will have a game for you!" He offered over his shoulder. Shani smiled back as his soldiers came over and hovered next to him. They all watched the odd, headstrong, doctor stride away with a renewed energy in every step.

Chapter 29

Colonel Moss was an amiable man who made sure those under him knew they all came from the same place; and that egos were not to be tolerated in the military machine. He treated men and women as equally as possible given the protocol of the hierarchy, and in return he was loved and respected for his fairness. It was because of this that Shani felt he could call on the Colonel regarding the doctor's request.

Moss had listened respectfully and immediately responded with delight. "It's inspiring because it's so ludicrous," he replied.

"And I remembered your words, Colonel," returned Shani, "Never dismiss an idea outright no matter how outrageous it may seem at first."

The more they talked about it, the more they decided the boulder needed to go and a game needed to happen. And why not! Was it not the playing fields where great nations sent their best athletes to compete for championships and bragging rights? If they managed it correctly, the game would be a brilliant historical victory; of course, if it failed it would be a horrific historical nightmare. It was madness but a good madness, and exactly what was needed. Just the thought of something like this succeeding put a smile on both of their faces. But first they needed to address the task at hand... how to remove the boulder.

Moss agreed to make a few calls to the right people. He was known for rolling a soccer ball under his foot as he engaged others on the phone. It was his way of keeping calm and finding the right words to convince, strategize, and organize. Some men fiddled with worry beads, some squeezed rubber balls, and others played with fidget spinners; Colonel Moss toyed with a ball under foot, and if it so pleased him, he would kick it against the wall as he wandered around his office carrying out his daily tasks. He loved soccer that much.

Moss and Shani eventually decided to treat getting rid of the boulder like an ordinance disposal mission. This way the colonel would not have to go through the normal, and ridiculously prolonged procedure needed for an incursion. The story would be that *someone* had reported another un-exploded shell near the school; and for all the right safety reasons, they needed it disposed of immediately. That it happened to be right next to the boulder in the soccer field was a happy coincidence. The location was remote enough that in the middle of the night no one would be around. To make certain, they would advise the right people. It would be an in and out mission, completed before the engines were even warm.

When Rami went to bed that night, his heart returned to its familiar heaviness. It had become customary for him to fear another night of either lying awake frustrated, or being shrouded in a heavy mantle of nightmares. Hassan would often enter his dreams —Hassan at all ages, which never made sense inside the dream; but the rules of nocturnal storytelling were all at play. He would see Hassan strapped in a suicide vest and disappear in a burst of pink mist. He would see the twelve-year-old Hassan lying on his bed listening to music, and then suddenly swallow a packet of bullets. Occasionally, the toddler Hassan would appear before him, struggling to carry the cinder block. That was the one image that always brought Rami joy, but when he awoke in the middle of the night, or in the morning, reality set in and that joy was instantly replaced by a deep, impenetrable sadness. Regardless, Rami could not fight his exhaustion and his eyes soon grew heavy, his breath becoming slow and labored.

Several miles away, on an Israeli airfield, two pilots scrambled to their gunships to perform their regular checklist before main rotors began to spin. As the blades chopped through the cool night air, the distant rumble of the engines reverberated across the flat, dry landscape. When they received clearance from the tower, the pilots slowly lifted up and flew towards their destination.

Rami began tossing in his sleep, his incoherent mumblings escaping his lips.

In the distance the helicopters remained low along the hilly terrain, their noses pointed slightly down as if sniffing the ground along the route.

Rami's barely audible rambling grew louder and more intense. Lyda sat up in bed. She was accustomed to Rami's midnight mumbling and would often quiet him until he appeared to return to a more restful state. But now she heard something above that frightened her. It was never good to hear gunships in the middle of the night, especially not this close.

As the gunships approached the village, they ascended into the darkness where they had a better overall view of the landscape below. The lead pilot identified the school ahead and confirmed the target with his wingman.

In the bedroom, random words escaped Rami's mumbling lips as his head shook from left to right —an internal struggle in his world of dreams. Lyda's eyes drew upwards as the war birds flew right over the roof shuddering the house in their wake.

As the helicopters neared the schoolyard, their searchlights landed on the boulder, which stuck out like the sorest of thumbs in the middle of the flat pitch. The pilots maneuvered their birds to each corner at one end of the field, allowing them to aim their guns in the same direction. When the target was locked on their screens, the lead pilot gave the countdown and two rockets whistled quickly away to annihilate the boulder. A colossal explosion lit up the night sky, sending shards in every direction. The boulder was no more.

At the moment of impact, Rami bolted awake screaming like a child, his cries reverberating throughout the household. "Hassan! Hassan! How could I let you go? How could I lose you like this?"

Marwan had already jumped out of bed at the sound of the explosion and opened his bedroom door, with Rose following close behind. Lyda met them in the small cramped hallway,"It's okay," she whispered "They're not shooting at the village."

Marwan's concerned eyes looked towards his son's old room. "My brother...?"

"Just a bad dream," Lyda assured. "Nothing to worry about."

Marwan nodded respectfully, and he and Rose made their way back across the cold floor to the warmth of their bed.

Lyda returned to the room and wrapped her arms tightly around her husband. She felt him trembling as he began to cry. Cradling him, she leaned back against the headboard and drew him lovingly to her breast. "Shhh! Its ok my love; it's all right, my sweetest heart."

Rami clung to her like a child to his mother until his sobbing gradually subsided into a quiet whimper. Above them, the sound of the helicopters receded as the pilots veered back towards their base.

In his bedroom, Marwan and Rose lay wide-awake, still listening for more explosions and for whatever else was to come from Rami and Lyda's bedroom. They could hear the helicopters leaving but it did nothing to calm their rattled nerves. "I wish I could heal him," Marwan suddenly uttered as he pulled the sheets closer to his chest.

Rose looked at him sympathetically and wound her arm through his. "Healing will come in its own time; in its own way."

In the darkness, Marwan placed his hand on top of hers and closed his eyes. "I hope so," he replied.

As the morning light began to peek in through the window, Lyda woke and discovered that, for the first time in years, she and Rami had fallen asleep holding each other. She sat quietly in thought, pushing away the usual sadness of the morning — the customary heartache of parental grief —and focused on the new feeling that was now sitting with her; the promise of a new day. For the first time since Hassan's death, she hadn't awakened with tears in her eyes. She couldn't fully comprehend it, but there was no guilt attached to looking forward to whatever the day might bring. It was a good beginning just to wake up next to her husband. She leaned forward and gently kissed his forehead. He was a good man with an honest heart. He deserved more. Without disturbing him, she sunk further down into the sheets, and held him closer.

Chapter 30

When Rami woke, no words were spoken between him and Lyda. Holding on tightly to one another in bed was something that they had not done in as long as either could remember. That it lasted as long as it did was a pure indication of how deeply they had missed each other. They could hear Marwan and Rose rustling around in the kitchen and, before long, the rich aroma of coffee drifted in.

"We should get up," Rami finally said.

"We should," returned Lyda.

But neither of them budged until Marwan gently knocked on the door, urging them to breakfast.

In the bathroom Rami studied himself in the mirror and was surprised at how relaxed he looked; his back seemed less hunched — his brow less heavy. It was as if a huge weight had been lifted from his shoulders. Hassan was gone. The loss of their son had changed their lives forever, but for the first time since his arrival, Rami felt hopeful that he and Lyda's relationship would heal; and because of his morning with her, he would always remember this day as the turning point.

After a leisurely breakfast with his family, Rami walked up the hill toward the school, his mind preoccupied with thoughts of his wife. As he approached the pitch still lost in thought, his eyes settled on one tiny rock after another until he realized something was different. Looking up, he took in the vast crater where the boulder had once stood. He squinted to see if he was in fact seeing what he thought he was seeing. Then he remembered the vague rattle of gunships that had disturbed his sleep in the middle of the night, and everything became clear. "That son of a gun," he said out loud.

As he entered the classroom, he could see the residual damage done by the rocket fire. The few windows that had panes were blown out, and shattered glass sparkled in the morning light across the floor. Excited, Rami hurried to his desk and began to formulate another plan to get the children back in school.

It took some convincing, but Rami finally managed to get the children to meet him at the fountain. Since the tragedy of Yasser's death, many of them felt guilty knowing that if they had been in school that day he might still be with them. Rami wished to alleviate their pain while encouraging them to move forward.

"I've asked you to come here today because my offer of an education still stands, but the deal has sweetened." Everyone looked intrigued. "Follow me!"

Rami remained silent while the children peppered him with questions as he led them up the hill. When they arrived at the field, everyone stood dumbfounded, gazing at the crater.

"How did you do this?" Rafik marveled.

Walking over to the nearest stone, Rami picked it up, held it for everyone to see, and then threw it off the pitch. "These stones do not belong on our playing field, so the first thing we have to do is get rid of them!" *Surely the symbolism would not be lost on them*, Rami thought, as each child picked up the nearest rock and threw it away. Rami pushed over a wheel barrel to be loaded with the chunks of rock that were too big to toss. "And we can put the bigger ones in here."

Once the wheelbarrow was full, a few of the boys wheeled it over to the edge of the crater and dumped in the rocks.

"We must also fill in the holes that have been left behind," Rami added. It took several hours, but finally the crater was filled and covered over with dirt, which they had collected from around the grounds; and every hole, large and small, had been smoothed over.

"That's a job well done, everyone! Now, follow me into the school!" Rami walked briskly towards the building. A collective sigh rose up, but no one protested. "We have to change the way we look at things," he stated as he passed out brooms. Everyone began sweeping up the broken glass and debris strewn across the floor. "We have to look at the world through new eyes." He ushered everyone over to the glassless windows, and had them look out at the smooth, clear field. "The consequences of team work," he said smiling.

Walking over to the blackboard, he drew a line down the center and outlined the lesson for the day on one side but left the other side blank. "Once we take care of this side of the blackboard..." he pointed to the history lesson, "...then we can take care of this side." He pointed to the right side where he drew the rectangle of a soccer field, and within it marked X's and 0's indicating teams.

The children gathered around him, buzzing with enthusiasm as they quibbled about who would play what position.

"So, I just have one question for you?" Rami said, which quieted them all abruptly. "Who's in?"

Every child's hand shot up in the air joined by a chorus of, "Me, me, me!" Rami smiled and began jotting down names on the blackboard.

Later that day during practice, the new teammates powered across the unobstructed field with glowing faces as they ran drills. Rami and Omar watched from the sidelines, blowing their whistles and barking out directives.

When Rami walked into his class the following day, he was startled to discover it overflowing with additional students. He looked over at Rafik who sat proudly in the front row. 'What is this?' Rami asked.

"Word has spread that we are playing against the Israelis," stated Rafik proudly.

Rami was surprised. He hadn't had a chance to address the topic with the children and already the word was out. "Yes, but there is no promise of that," replied Rami, eyeing the eager faces surrounding him. "I have not been given a date, a time, or confirmation that it will even take place."

"But there is a possibility?" Rafik continued.

'Well, perhaps... but...' Rami chose his words cautiously as excitement circulated throughout the room. "...but right now, I am here to teach!"

"And we are here to learn!" yelled one of the new boys, whose declaration was met with agreement by all.

Rami eyed them doubtfully. *This is too good to be true*, he thought, deciding to test their genuineness. "There will be homework and tests. This is a *real* school. You do understand that if your grades are not good, neither are your prospects for making the team?"

"We were barely half a team before, but now we even have substitutes," Rafik returned, smiling broadly and nodding along with his friends. "We're not going to do anything to spoil that!"

Rami was satisfied. Removing his jacket, he rolled up his sleeves. "Okay. Well let's get to learning then, shall we?" As he turned to the blackboard, Lyda appeared in the doorway with a basket of lunch. She stopped short, looking at the full class, then at her husband, then at her basket, which she now realized was woefully inadequate. Rami smiled lovingly as his wife turned right back around with an overwhelmed but playful sigh.

Chapter 31

Christine sat on the creaky bed of her hotel room typing on her laptop. She had become accustomed to the constant sputtering of the overused fan and weird smells drifting in from the hallway. It wasn't the first time she had to put up with poor accommodations and it certainly wouldn't be the last.

Vacillating between a host of creased napkins and her notepad, she tried to finish her latest story. She paused for a moment to stretch, and stared out at the early evening sky. It was still light out even though the sun had set, and she found herself marveling at the beauty that could be found in any pocket of the world.

When a buzzing alerted her to an incoming call, she picked up her phone to find Melinda's photo on the screen. As was her habit lately, she hesitated and thought about not answering but then reconsidered. "Hi!" She waited for the response but the silence on the other end was longer than usual. "Mel? Are you ok?" Melinda was there —Christine could hear her breathing.

"I'm fine, but you'll never believe what happened."

Christine stood up, poised to pack her bags if necessary. 'I'm listening."

"When I came home from the weekend at my parents, there were muddy tire tracks all over the lawn next door. I didn't think much of it until I went inside to put away groceries. Then, I looked out of the back window. I couldn't believe it!"

"Couldn't believe what? You're keeping me in suspense," Christine urged impatiently.

"The pool is gone!"

Christine was silent for a moment, and then slumped down onto the bed. "What do you mean?"

"Charlie had it filled in over the weekend."

Christine fell back against her pillow at the mention of their neighbor's name. Charlie had always seemed an amiable man whenever she'd run into him, which wasn't often as she was frequently away on assignment. Melinda, on the other hand, had become well acquainted with him over the years, and a casual friendship had developed —the two often drinking morning coffees together and chatting about their errands for the day. Charlie's bad back had come up more than once in these conversations, and Mel had suggested swimming as a remedy. Excited by the idea, and noting that his back yard was big enough to accommodate a pool, he decided to hire a contractor.

Months later, with the pool complete, all that remained was the perimeter fencing, which sat in rolls by the cedar hedge that separated their properties. The contractor was supposed to erect the fence the day the pool was filled with water, but a last-minute emergency called him away. That was the morning their son, Jack, had awoken early. Without a sound, the three-year old found his way into the back yard and spotted the sparkling water through the hedges. By the time Mel went to wake up their only child, it was too late.

The heartbreak was unimaginable and the whole neighborhood felt it —the weight of tragedy equaled only by Charlie's guilt and sense of responsibility. Christine was able to distance herself from the whole ordeal by disappearing into her work, while poor Melinda had to live with the aftermath, occasionally running into her devastated neighbor and seeing the empty pool every time she looked out of their back windows. She and Charlie barely spoke anymore, understandably so.

"Chris? Did you hear me?"

Melinda's voice jolted Christine back to the present. "Wow!" she replied, not knowing what else to say.

Melinda began to weep. "Yeah... and I was curious, so I snuck over there last night..." she sniffed, "Oh Chris! Charlie planted an oak tree sapling where the pool was, and at the base there is a plaque that reads: *Jackson Cooper. Forever.*"

"Wow!" Christine repeated, choking back her tears.

"I know. It was so sweet. So… special."

Another long silence followed as Christine tried to wrap her mind around Charlie's gesture.

"Are you still there?" Melinda asked after a moment. Nothing. "Christine?"

"It's all a bit overwhelming," Christine answered, blowing her nose. "I wish I was there with you right now, Mel. I just want to hold you and talk about this properly."

"Yeah, I wish the same," Melinda replied.

Christine hesitated, and then breathed in deeply. "There's more to say. Something happened the other day, and I'm having a hard time with it."

"I'm listening," Melinda said softly.

In the following days, soccer practice took on a new intensity continuing until sundown —far longer than the promised hour after school. Several of the parents began attending to cheer the team on, and the field quickly became the new town square with people mingling, gossiping, and debating while drinking coffee and tea from well-worn thermoses. When the long shadows reached across the dry earth and the falling light all but disappeared, the silhouettes lingered until all adrenaline dissipated, and the last few stragglers slowly ambled home.

By the end of the week Rami was exhausted. He sat at his usual table at Marwan's café, his body drained, when Marwan placed a plate in front of him. Rami looked up at his brother and then down at the plate and gave them both a sniff.

"What is this?"

"*This* is my famous French omelet," Marwan replied, laying down a knife and fork.

"But I didn't order..." Marwan held up his hand, sat beside him, and waited silently, staring at the plate.

Finally relenting, Rami picked up his fork and took a bite. The omelet was perfection —smooth and evenly cooked with no embellishments. It melted onto his tongue filling his stomach with warmth. He smiled and nodded his approval. "Why do you call it a French omelet?"

"It sounds more *high end.*"

'What's in it?"

"Nothing but fresh eggs and butter. Simple is better." Marwan moved his chair closer; there were other things on his mind. "Listen, I've been thinking."

Taking another bite, Rami regarded his brother warily.

"Do you know what *you* need?" Marwan did not wait for an answer. "A sponsor!"

Rami choked on his mouthful, "A what?"

"A sponsor! You know... someone who supports the team financially. Every team needs a sponsor!" Marwan proclaimed.

"We don't need a sponsor!" Rami stated quickly, wiping his mouth on a napkin.

"Sure, you do. And I spoke to that journalist lady —that reporter —and told her, and..."

"Wait!" Rami interrupted. "You told her about the game?" He was obviously annoyed, but Marwan's growing excitement could not be culled.

"Why yes! This is big news. Don't you realize how historic this is? That lady journalist said..."

"Christine Cooper."

"Yes, Christine Cooper said she'll promote it and then shoot it live. It could be seen all over the world!"

"Have you lost your mind? This is a simple game of football between the children. It's low-key for security reasons. If the Israelis' hear about Ms. Cooper they may not show up at all!" Rami was livid and pushed the plate away.

Marwan looked at the partially eaten omelet and felt deflated for a moment. "This is a much bigger deal than a simple game between a few kids," he said, looking over at a cluster of cardboard boxes sitting on the floor. Then after a beat, his jovial tone returned. "Anyway, I was thinking we could at least get them some uniforms."

"Uniforms?" Rami's brow furrowed. Marwan was not going to give up easily. "Where are we going to get uniforms?"

Marwan pushed over one of the boxes with his foot and pulled out a handful of white T-shirts. "Well, not exactly uniforms but these shirts could all say the same thing."

"Which is?"

"Marwan's Café! Or maybe *Marwan's Palace*, or maybe just, *Marwan's.*"

"This is ridiculous. We don't need a sponsor and we certainly don't need the whole world knowing about the game." Just as those words came out of his mouth, Rami began to question the justification of his last statement. Marwan seemed to read his mind.

"That is *exactly* what we need —the world to watch! They only know of the killing and hatred!" After a pause he added, "This will be good for our... how do they say it? —our brand!"

Rami stared at his brother in astonishment, and then his lips broke into a smile. "You've been going on the internet again, haven't you?" He said playfully, but Marwan didn't bite.

"Well, like it or not, I've already been your sponsor, you just don't know it!"

Rami looked at his brother curiously.

"Ok, for example, Lyda has been making lunch for you and the children every day, and you used to say her cooking was terrible!"

"It was never *terrible*, but it has improved of late. Yes." Rami conceded.

"All of a sudden? That's because I help her make the hummus and fresh tahini dressing from scratch. And who do you think gives her this and that when she runs out? Pita, tomatoes, olive oil, herbs... they all come from my stock."

"I didn't give it much thought. I guess I've been too..."

"And there are more kids now that need to eat and keep up their strength. I have already increased my supplies to accommodate this!" Marwan sat back and folded his arms.

Rami shook his head, returning to the subject. "This is getting to be too much —TV coverage, team shirts, sponsorship ads. What's next? I'm telling you; we can't make a big thing about this. They will call it off. Actually, maybe I should call it..."

"No!" Marwan shouted. "You can't call it off, and I won't let you!"

Rami was startled by his brother's intensity.

"Look…" Marwan continued, softening his tone, "…this is a good thing you are doing. These kids are excited. I have not seen them look forward to something like this in a… well I have just not seen it. So, don't take it away from them! Please!" Marwan began folding and stuffing the shirts back in the box. Within seconds he had transitioned back into the strong, scolding older brother that Rami had often acquiesced to in his youth. As he watched Marwan rise and push the box towards the others, he let his brother's words fully sink in.

Chapter 32

Rami's classroom was now at full capacity, and the children had begun to take as much interest in what they were being taught, as they were in the soccer practice that proceeded it. Aside from engaging in discussions about equality, diplomacy, and social change, Rami's pupils took to grilling him on Jewish culture, and in which ways it resembled their own. The prospect of meeting Israeli peers who shared their love of soccer excited everyone, even though Rami continued to maintain an air of skepticism as to whether the game would even come to fruition. Still, he had to believe that Shani was a man of his word. He answered everyone's questions as best he could and continued to scribble his thoughts on conflict management across the board.

One afternoon, in the middle of a lesson, a distant rumbling of engines drew everyone's attention to the window. Rafik rushed over first, followed by his friends who all competed for a space to watch, as a host of vehicles appeared over the rise.

"What is it? What's all the noise?" Rami asked.

"Israelis!" Rafik's eyes remained fixed on the spectacle in front of him. "They are taking up positions on both sides of the field!"

Rami's breath stopped short; the IDF's appearance could only mean one thing; Shani had come through. "It's on!" he declared, a broad smile stretching across his face.

In unison, the children turned their attention to their teacher and the world seemed to freeze. Then, as if wound up again from a pause in the earth's rotation, they scrambled madly over each other and flung themselves through the door, running out onto the field.

In the village, Christine and Greg were walking to their van when an Israeli tank drove past them and headed up the hill towards the school. Christine looked behind her to where another tank sat surrounded by soldiers who were busy setting up checkpoints. "I wonder what's going on," she said, looking at Greg.

"Maybe it's the game?" Greg replied. They smiled knowingly at each other and quickened their pace.

"They should let us through without a hitch, I've already spoken to the authorities about filming the match." Christine climbed into the passenger's seat and took out two small press cards from her satchel.

"Show time!" replied Greg, putting his keys into the ignition.

Marwan wandered out in front of his café when he heard the tank's deep roar. He looked down one side of the road and then the other. "Now what? No matter... this is going to be bad for business!" He turned back to his café wringing the rag in his hands. After a moment, he came back out and looked up towards the school. Flinging off his apron, he tossed the rag onto the nearest table, grabbed the box of T-shirts, and hurriedly made his way to the field.

In the Israeli settlement nearby, Colonel Moss's soccer team was dressed in shiny new, green uniforms, and waiting patiently near an army transport. One parent of each child was allowed to attend the game; everyone else was to remain behind for security reasons. Parents wished their children luck before the soldiers lifted them one by one into the back of the truck. Family members waved goodbye, some through tears and others with concerned faces; although they knew their loved ones were in good hands, their safety could never be fully guaranteed. Still, the game offered a bridge of sorts between communities, and for this reason alone the parents had consented.

Back at the school, Israeli soldiers marked the field in a grid pattern and walked around methodically swinging metal detectors over every square inch. Rami's team stayed off to the side, watching, stretching, and working out plays, the air rife with excitement.

The Israeli convoy made its way onto the road and began its journey towards the school. Led by three armed Humvees, the transport carrying the team and their parents was followed by several more armed vehicles, which made for an imposing sight.

When they approached the Beit Jbal checkpoint, they were allowed straight through, while civilians who were eagerly waiting for permission to pass were left to watch in frustration.

The convoy raised a cloud of dust as it raced by open fields, passing a lone farmer who looked up from his work to watch. When the vehicles disappeared around the bend, the man reached into his pocket and drew out a phone.

In a crude building nearby —a simple rectangle of cinderblocks sporting a dirt floor — Moustache listened intently, hung up his cell phone, and nodded to his accomplices. Several unkempt young men returned to their task of strapping an explosive belt onto... *Zara.*

The convoy continued along the road and was soon joined by two gunships flying half a kilometer ahead. A shepherd stood on a path cut into the side of the hill to see what had rattled his herd of goats. Covering his sun-damaged face as the dust rose, he watched the convoy below pass, and then coaxed his herd back together, driving them higher towards fertile ground. "The further away we are from that spectacle, the better!" He muttered, shaking his head uneasily.

Back in the small cinderblock building, Moustache stood in front of Zara and regarded her with pride. The girl was nervous and sweating, fear evident in her eyes. The rest of the men stood around her in a circle —a ritual they had performed dozens of times in the past —as they acknowledged her sacrifice without remorse or compassion.

"This is a glorious day for you… for us… for Allah! You will never be forgotten by us, or by them!" Moustache declared. Zara wiped the sweat from her brow and nodded. "This is our opportunity to impact and horrify! The world will soon shudder at our very name!" Moustache and his collective had been waiting too long, like a dormant virus under the skin; but now their time had come.

"Yes, the world would soon know us all!" His men agreed amongst themselves. No one would ever imagine that such an audacious act of terror would occur so close to home, and among their own people; but if there were losses on their side, so be it. The fallout was outweighed by the impact the incident would have on the world stage.

As the convoy rolled through the village, people excitedly dropped what they were doing and began following on foot, making their way up to the school.

At the makeshift entrance, everyone was stopped and thoroughly searched. Christine and Greg had produced their press cards in an attempt to expedite their entry, but they were searched and questioned like everyone else before being allowed through.

Greg hurried on to survey the area to determine where best to set up his camera, while Christine quickly scanned the field. Her eyes landed on Rami who was standing amidst the boys as they practiced kicking the ball back and forth. Rami felt her gaze and looked over, regarding her curiously with a nod. The air felt electric as the magnitude of the *little game* began to take hold.

Zara wound her way down a steep slope along a patch of scraggly akoub bushes. Once she ascended the next knoll, she could see the village and the schoolyard perched atop the hill behind it. Her heart began to race as the reality of the mission sunk in. She stopped and remembered her coaching. They had told her to always remain calm and not appear suspicious in any way. If her nerves got the better of her and she appeared to be sweating unusually, or her breathing was labored, the soldiers would be on to her. "Focus on the mission, not your nerves!" Moustache had said. "Israeli soldiers are trained to spot both the obvious and discreet signs that accompany a martyr. If you fail to keep your composure, you will be captured, jailed, and tortured or shot on the spot. You will die without glory!"

She kept repeating all that she was told, but her nerves were getting away from her. In the past, she had run on these hills with ease; but on this day, the air was heavy in her lungs and it pushed out against her chest. "Calm down!" She muttered. "Calm down! You are about to die a glorious death."

When Marwan finally made it through the entrance —his cardboard box still intact —he rushed over to the boys and pulled out the T-shirts for them to wear. The children looked at the clothing as if they were rags. "Yes, they are not perfect," said Marwan smiling broadly, "...but they are still a uniform of sorts and that will make you feel even more of a team."

Rafik pulled one of the T-shirts over his head and straightened it out around his small frame. As he turned around, Rami could see *Marwan's Café,* handwritten in marker on the back. Rami could only shake his head in embarrassed disbelief.

Chapter 33

As the army transport rattled and hummed along, the Israeli team ensconced inside was beginning to feel the excitement of their adventure. This transcended to both the parents and soldiers sitting with them who could not contain their nervous smiles, as the steady chopping of the propellers from the gunships above added to their sense of security. From their seated positions, the group bounced a football back and forth with their knees until the transport began to make its way up the slow incline towards the field. Everyone stood up and hung on to the upper bars, their hearts fluttering in anticipation.

Rami's team, *Yasser's Arsenal,* which the children had named themselves, gathered around him as they watched the truck make its way to the goal posts. Just ahead of it, Cohen pulled up in a jeep carrying Shani in the passenger seat, and two more soldiers in the back. Invigorated by the pending event, Shani jumped out of the jeep and strode to Rami's side, a soccer ball in his hands. "Dr. Amar! Hard to believe it, but here we are."

Rami smiled. "I don't know what to say, Major, other than thank you." He regarded the children by his side. "We are all grateful that you found a way to make this happen."

"You made this happen, Doctor! I simply relayed your idea to a man who loves the game."

Rafik and his friends stared up at the formidable Israeli in front of them with uncertainty in their eyes. The Major smiled at Rafik. "And what position do you play, young man?"

Rafik looked at Rami who nodded. "I'm the Captain and striker," he answered proudly.

Shani leaned down and passed Rafik the shiny new football. "Well Captain, this is going to be a different game than expected; but as the leader, I know you will encourage your team to do what is proposed." Rafik's eyes widened in wonder. Shani straightened.

"Dr. Amar, after Colonel Moss considered the fairness of such a game, and the competitiveness that exists between teams, he believed mixing our players would be the best option."

Rami was taken aback, and turned to Marwan who was now standing by his side.

"You mean have Arabs and Jews on the same team?" asked Marwan incredulously. "Do the parents of your players know?"

"My brother has a point, Major." Rami nodded to the growing crowd of spectators who were now sitting on bleachers set up by the soldiers. "These people came to root for their team. I'm not sure how they will react to this news."

"That is why you should be the one to tell them." The major stood aside to reveal a small podium and microphone being set up in front of the crowd. "As you have repeatedly demonstrated, you are quite persuasive, Doctor."

Rami looked at the podium and crowd again, and for the first time noticed Greg, camera on shoulder, filming him. Christine was standing within listening range — notebook in hand. As Greg moved in closer, the Israeli team disembarked from their transport, their crisp green uniforms striking in the sunlight.

Rami's team tugged at their amateurish shirts and looked on with envy. Colonel Moss's team, *The United*, looked back with equal curiosity, eyeing the clothing of their rivals, and whispering nervously among themselves.

"Oh boy, oh boy… are we in trouble!" quipped Omar wheeling over to Rami's side. "And where is Zara? She's supposed to be here!"

"Wow, look at them!" Fatima said to the air.

"Nice uniforms!" Rafik noted.

Rami looked at everyone's discouraged faces. "How you dress is not what wins game," he reminded everyone.

Rafik's chest expanded. "It's how you play, that counts!"

"Correct!" Rami turned to Shani. "I presume the children you send to us will wear our shirts without complaint?"

"Since shirt swapping is common practice at the end of the game, I doubt they will object." The Major's' eyes returned to Rafik. "And you, young man… as captain, you will choose which of your players will join the other team. I expect you to be fair and professional."

Rafik's chest puffed out again, and with a quick nod he gathered his team around him.

"I will go and speak with our team's captain. Now might be a good time to address the crowd, Doctor Amar. They appear to be getting restless." The Major was about to turn away when he stopped. "Whatever you chose to say to them, let it have a calming effect. This game can still be cancelled before the whistle is blown."

Marwan slapped a hand on his brother's shoulder. "My brother could convince a donkey to lay eggs, Major!"

Shani held back a smile. He didn't trust Marwan a stitch. In fact, he had kept him under surveillance for years, but the man certainly oozed crude charm. "On that score, I do believe you," he replied. He turned back to Rami. "We've come a long way since your arrival, Doctor. You have caused me both irritation and reflection." Rami's eyebrows rose. "I am grateful to you for both." Without waiting for a response, Shani nodded cordially and briskly strode away, leaving Rami alone with Marwan.

"Odd little man," Marwan said, as he watched the Major head to the bus.

"Not odd... complicated," returned Rami. "And... hardly *little*.

"He's little in comparison to me," replied Marwan.

Rami eyed his brother's generous belly. "Everyone's little in comparison to you."

As Rami headed to the podium, Marwan looked down at his belly and sighed. "True," he answered.

Already, the heat had taken its toll on the underarms of Rami's linen jacket. As he approached the podium, he took it off, but not before producing his trusted white handkerchief from one of its pockets. The crowd had grown three sizes from when the first spectators had arrived, and as they buzzed and squirmed on their hard seats, Rami had a difficult time placing any of their faces. Then, Lyda came into view. She was sitting beside Rose, mid-center, staring warmly at her husband. Rami was immediately calmed by her presence. She smiled at him lovingly before raising her own white handkerchief to her brow and gently dabbing.

Rami looked down at the large cotton swathe in his hands. Lyda had embroidered his initials in one of the corners but it had become faded and frayed with time. He felt the slightly raised thread between his fingers and smiled. He still relied on this piece of material to cool him, to offer respite, to combat the unbearable heat and restore, even temporarily, a sense of peace. Looking back up, the crowd had now settled into a murmur, all eyes on him, expecting, waiting. Rami returned to the handkerchief, stretched it out, and wiped his brow. Clearing his throat, he pulled the microphone toward him.

"Hello everyone. Ahem… today is… today is not like any other day in Beit Jbal." The crowd's murmurs grew. "Today is a day of… of celebration!"

He looked across the mass of hot and irritated faces.
He was already losing them

"Why hasn't the game started?" Someone
cried from the back of the bleachers. "Why are the
Jews stalling?" A few people raised their voices in
agreement, and the Israeli parents who were now
walking towards the stands began to look worried.
Rami lifted his hand with the handkerchief, and a
sudden breeze caught the material. Surprisingly the
crowd settled.

"Today is a day of celebration, because today
Palestinians and Israeli's work together to forge a new path for
our children's futures." Rami looked at Lyda, who smiled and
nodded, encouraging him on. "Today, Palestinian and Israeli
children will play on the same teams, supporting each other...
encouraging each other..." A loud murmur sprouted amongst
the villagers. Lyda was now looking at Rose, surprise etched on
both of their faces. Rami did not wait; looking at the fluttering
swathe between his fingers, he extended his arm higher.
"This..." he said, and the crowd quieted again; "...This looks to
be nothing more than a piece of white cloth, but over the years
it has symbolized many things — the purity of our deeds; the
act of surrender; even grief and mourning —a reminder of our
hard-fought effort. Today, while we watch our children play,
while we support all of their efforts and recognize their

innocence amidst our strife, let it only represent one thing… the path to peace!"

The silence was deafening. Rami's arm remained in position, the handkerchief in his hand dancing as the warm breeze picked up. *Perhaps I should have chosen my words more carefully*, he thought to himself, as he looked on at the sea of ruminating faces before hm. Then, a harsh whisper nearby caught his attention.

"Greg, over there! Close in on her hand!"

Rami's eyes followed Christine's pointing finger, and then Greg's camera, as it settled on the middle of the stands. Lyda's arm was up, her white handkerchief catching the same breeze as her husband. She looked at him with a mixture of love and determination filling her brimming eyes, and then stood up amidst the stillness, her gaze settling on the children behind him. Rose followed suit; followed by Marwan who, without a handkerchief to his name, held up one of the white T-shirts and turned towards the teams. More hands rose in the air as the atmosphere relaxed. The Israeli parents standing on the periphery, raised white kerchiefs, shirts, and scarves, whatever they had on hand that inferred their solidarity. The children felt the full impact of all the eyes on them. Rafik's chin rose as he directed his chosen peers to the other side of the pitch, and then received his new Israeli teammates with a genial nod, the crowd erupting into applause.

Rami stepped down from the podium and walked to Rafik's side as the opposing team began warming up. He smiled at the new members who had just joined them, their shirts already changed. They looked nervous and uncertain of their new teammates, but when Rafik called them into a huddle, they complied, their expressions changing to that of determined athletes.

Rami joined the huddle. "Play this game like the ladies and gentlemen you all are," he said staring into each player's eyes. "Play it for young Yasser and for all of the Palestinian and Israeli children who would have loved to be a part of this day but are no longer with us."

"And let us play for Hassan," Omar interjected. The team looked over at him as he sat proudly in his wheelchair.

Rami was touched by the sentiment. "Yes. Thank you, Omar!"

Everyone leaned further in to their huddle, and with hand over hand, they shouted, "Let's go!" before high-fiving each other and hitting the field.

In the middle of the pitch, one of two soldiers acting as referee flipped a coin. The game was officially on. *The United* won the toss, and chose their goal. Fatima moved to center to kickoff. She was by far the strongest kicker in Yasser's *Arsenal*, and lofted the ball deep into the opposing team's territory. Dust immediately rose up and accentuated the shafts of sunlight, which cut through the field, as *The United* charged forward. When the two teams collided, a flurry of feet jabbed away in a mad scramble for possession of the ball.

While the crowd cheered, Greg captured the action on his camera and Christine remained glued to her phone. She had decided to relay the game to Melinda, but was having some difficulty getting through. When the first goal was scored, she dropped her phone in excitement, scribbled down a few notes, and then picked the phone back up only to realize that she had lost the connection and had to restart the process of getting through all over again. She would bookend the video with her own thoughts and a few interviews after Greg finished filming. But for now, she had enough material to write a riveting story, and she wanted to share that information with the woman she loved.

Zara made her way along a narrow strip of backyards and alleys, instinctively staying out of sight until she finally reached the edge of the road leading to the school. The checkpoint was teeming with soldiers. A substantial number of villagers had already been allowed through, so the lineup was short, but the soldiers remained vigilant, their eyes peeled along the road for anything suspicious. Zara's legs refused to carry her forward. Backing away, she found a small resting place between two adjoining walls, and there she lay in wait beneath an explosion of bougainvillea.

At the game, the ball was skillfully passed back and forth across the field, and, narrowly avoiding an interception, was once again kicked into *The United's* territory. The Israelis on both teams were fast on their feet and notably talented.

"Look at them go!" Shouted Omar as the crowd grew louder. "They're so good! But Fatima is better!"

Rami smiled; Fatima was only thirteen, but tall and strong, and there was something in her gait and smile that reminded him of Lyda. Omar and Zara would often wait for her after class and walk home together. Omar and Fatima were becoming inseparable. *Hassan would be happy to know that his friend is alive and well,* thought Rami. *And that he likes a girl.* Rami felt a sense of peace wash over him.

One more pass and Fatima kicked the ball hard, but it ricocheted off the goalpost. The crowd reacted with a collective sigh, distracting Christine who was still attempting to video call Melinda. A few flickers and Melinda's image finally cut through the static. Christine held the phone up in front of her.

"Hi!"

"Hi sweetheart!"

"I've been trying to reach you forever! I want to show you something." Christine reversed the camera on her phone so that Melinda could see the game in progress.

Melinda wasn't sure what she was seeing at first until the choppy imagery stabilized. "Wow! Those kids look like they're having a blast!

"They are! Palestinian and Israeli kids — playing together on *both* teams!" Shouted Christine above the cries of the crowd. "Can you believe it? It's such a great story! Oh, Mel... I can't wait to share it with you!"

"I can't wait to hear it, Chris."

Christine held the phone up closer and looked at her wife lovingly. "I'm coming home next weekend. I've already booked the flight. I love you."

From her camouflaged vantage point, Zara could see the game being played up on the hill. There it was —her short future laid out before her. She desperately tried to regain her breath, her courage, and most importantly, her composure. The hardest part of this mission was yet to come. "Calm down," she whispered, "Calm down!" and she wiped a trickle of sweat from her forehead with her arm.

On the field, Rafik was arguing with the referee about a penalty call he had received. Some spectators raised their voices in annoyance, which added to the tension. Rami quickly intervened; "Get your focus back into the game, Rafik!" He said, pointing to the other children on the pitch. "Remember what's important here." Rami half-expected Rafik to storm off the field in his usual manner, but Rafik surprised him.

"Yes, coach!"

What a long way this boy has come, thought Rami as Rafik ran back out onto the field, ... *and, in such a short period of time.*

Zara reclaimed her resolve and began to breathe evenly in preparation. With a dry mouth and a scratchy throat, she whispered, "My beloved God. I am here for you. I do this for you and for Palestine!" Her mind began to detach when she suddenly heard voices growing louder. A small group of villagers and farmers were making their way to the game chatting and laughing. This was her chance; she would walk among them through the checkpoint, answering the soldier's questions diligently and with all the composure she could muster. The soldiers were unlikely to search each member of the group unless their suspicion was aroused. Then, it would only be a few more minutes until... *paradise.* "This is it!" She murmured. "My life is this moment and nothing more. I'll make sure you're not in my path, Omar, my cousin, you have suffered enough."

As Zara thought of Omar, her world seemed to shift into slow motion. She imagined the game on the field being played at this pace —slowly and deliberately where everything took longer than it should —the ball spinning through the air; soft grains of dust rising up; and shafts of sunlight flickering gently across the pitch. She watched as a drop of sweat fell from her brow and landed with a loud, reverberating plop at her feet. Then, the beat of her heart took over —pounding like a kettledrum in her ears —*boom, boom, boom!* She began to think about running away —finding herself a hiding place in the mountains —sustaining herself with dried insects and shrubs; but before she could imagine anything further, a sudden breeze found its way to her hiding place, rustling the bougainvillea and quickly drying her forehead. All of her thoughts vanished, and her heart slowed. Allowing the breeze to carry her, she drifted out onto the road and fluidly blended in with the others walking to the game.

Rami watched Rafik's breakaway in wonder. The small boy charged the goaltender and kicked the ball straight into the net.

"GOAL!" Shouted Rafik, his fists raised high in the air as villagers and parents erupted into cheers.

Someone tapped Rami's shoulder, and he turned to find Yasser's father standing behind him, his eyes brimming with tears. "I want to thank you, Doctor!" He drew in closer. "I want to thank you! I gave you a hard time, but now I understand what you were trying to do. I only wish… I only wish my boy was here." Before Rami could respond, Yasser's father had rejoined the crowd, emphatically cheering Yasser's friends on, the tears falling freely down his cheeks.

Rami smiled sadly and returned his gaze to the field. Major Shani stood off to one side with his corporal. Both seemed engrossed in the game.

"Today there are no Israeli's or Palestinians," said Marwan, nodding towards the Major as he walked to Rami's side.

"If only it would last," replied Rami.

"This is what we all needed," returned Marwan. "… a glimpse of what is possible."

Rami nodded. "I wish Hassan could have seen this."

"Yes," agreed Marwan, "And Imad" and he placed a warm hand on his brother's back, before his eyes returned to the game.

Zara had tried to come to terms with her destiny but was failing. Her body shuddered —her entire being acutely aware of everything around her. At first, she kept pace with the small crowd, which hummed along excitedly towards the checkpoint; but her nerves started to get the better of her as the villagers began to fall into line. Dropping back, her head rattled with the words, *Allah!* How often had she heard those words as she was growing up? *Allah Akbar! God is great!* They were benevolent words spoken during celebration —offered by neighbors and friends as tidings of joy and good fortune. Now they were words that conjured up fear —a prelude to pain and horror. She stopped to take a deep breath, and as she did, a pair of strong hands yanked her off the road and flung her into the ditch.

Zara impulsively reached for the trigger on her belt but her hand was caught and held before she could detonate it. She looked up and saw a man with piercing dark eyes and a scarf covering the lower half of his face.

"Change of plan!" Her captor said. "Not today!"

Zara immediately recognized Imad's voice. When she realized she had not been captured but had, in fact, been rescued from her fate, she was so overcome with gratitude that she hugged Imad, her whole body shivering with relief.

"Easy, easy, you are still armed," Imad reminded her.

"Yes, of course," replied Zara releasing him.

Imad slowly unpacked Zara's belt and carefully placed each piece in a satchel.

"They changed their mind?" Zara asked.

"Something like that." Imad closed the satchel. "Now get out of here before anyone sees you!"

Zara nodded and scrambled towards the wall that ran the length of the village. When she was sure the soldiers couldn't see her, she rose to her feet and darted to an adjacent alley. Her eyes lifted to the hills beyond the village and the brilliant blue sky, so rich in color it almost took her breath away. She breathed in deeply and began to run toward the small home she shared with her family. She had convinced her parents not to go to the game. She knew exactly where they would be —her mother in the kitchen preparing soup for their evening meal, and her father working on the old Volkswagen next to the house. She couldn't keep Omar away from the game but decided if she made it that far, she would detonate in the stands. Now, gratitude for those she loved filled her chest. Perhaps her life had been spared for them … for now, anyway.

Imad made his way to the Moustache's hideout. Releasing Zara was going to cause him serious problems. He was not involved in the operation —he didn't believe it was a judicious move, and he had told Moustache as much. "Most of the village will be there," he had argued. "Friends… family. Too many of our own have already lost their lives! This is a betrayal of all we fight for!"

"This is too big of an opportunity for us," Moustache replied coldly.

"Something of this magnitude is not an opportunity," Imad returned. "It's a warning to remain beneath the radar. Your operation will be the end for all of us. The Israelis won't stop until every last one of us is exterminated —no trial, no jail, just shot on sight or taken away into the night and oblivion!"

"I am not interested in cowards. The girl will carry out her duty and bring greatness to our name!"

In that moment, Imad realized that Moustache only cared about making a name for himself, nothing more; and he would be quite content manipulating and using up the lives of every youth in the village to accomplish this. Egomaniacal leaders were sloppy in Imad's books; their lust for power clouded their judgment. He had a choice; he could either let the operation proceed, or he could veto it without their knowledge. Then, he would only have to contend with Moustache and his men —not the blood of the village and not the full wrath of the IDF. Afterwards, he would have to leave, of course. Forged paperwork would get him across the border from where he could make his way to Jordan and disappear. Truthfully, after Hassan's death, he had lost his taste for the lifestyle he was leading. Maybe his uncle Rami was right; maybe it wasn't too late. He checked his firearm and threw the satchel over his shoulder. He had two of his own men waiting for him. Moustache would never see it coming.

The game was tied. Boys and girls moved in a blur on the field, back and forth, kicking up dust within the shafts of sunlight as the golden hour settled. Sounds of laughter, cheers, and applause, filled Rami's ears. He looked again at the crowd of spectators, his wife, his brother, Christine, Shani, and his team of engrossed soldiers. *The strange dream I kept having was a premonition...* he thought. *It is no longer a dream.* The handkerchief in his hands fluttered as another breeze found its way to him. Leaving Marwan's side, he found a small area away from everyone, and kissed the swathe of cool, white cloth.

"For you, my son," he whispered, letting the kerchief go. The breeze lifted the cloth up; its corners rippling like a flag, before gently being carried away. Another cheer rose up from the crowd as Rami turned to join them.

Acknowledgments,

Like any endeavor we undertake, storytelling is rarely done alone. Although I wrote *White Flags*, there are several people I must acknowledge and thank for their multifaceted support in the creation of this book. First and foremost, I want to thank the most beautiful human being I've ever known, Rowena Campbell. Not only did she encourage me to tell both sides of this story in order to weave a more balanced and nuanced tale; she also inspired me to listen to opposite views openly and without judgment, allowing for a more empathic focus when writing. This is a woman whose love has no bounds, and conversations with her forced me to look deeply within, making me a better human being and therefore a better storyteller.

Uri Moss, my dear Israeli friend, who loved this story from the beginning, and whose personal experience with the IDF (Israeli Defense Forces), and life in general in Israel and on the kibbutz, helped me to authenticate many of the characterizations, while ~~and~~ fact-checking numerous points of reference with regards to how things would actually be.

Joanne Gibson, whose friendship goes back to my days living in Los Angeles and continues in New York and beyond. She has remained a good and close friend whose encouragement and support have been invaluable in the honing of my craft and in the raw talents I have yet to hone, as I work on myself each day.

Last but not least, to my dear friend, Rowena Woods, whom I have been able to reconnect with after so many years. She has acted as my greatest supporter and sharpest critic. She was my editor and completely reshaped my thoughts on what it means to be an adept writer. Through her kind critique and savvy writing skills, she repeatedly showed me how this story could and should be better. There is no doubt that her contribution to this novel has made it a hell of a lot clearer, more interesting, diverse, and satisfying in every possible way.

To my family and friends who wondered when I would someday get a real job, though never saying it out loud... thank you for always being there for me. Without my family, I am lost and homeless in the worst possible sense. In that, I would never be able to ground myself in an ever-challenging and often-struggling world. You, family, are where grace, hope, and love reside.

ABOUT THE AUTHOR

Jo Marr is a writer, director, producer, musician & author whose career began when a substitute teacher showed the film, "The Making of Butch Cassidy & the Sundance Kid". He hadn't seen the actual movie itself but he immediately fell in love with the magic of movies.

Jo started as a background actor on movies such as "Sea of Love " & "Dream Team" learning by watching up close, legends like Al Pacino and Michael Keaton. When the California sunshine lured him away from the cold Canadian winters, he paid his dues coming up through the Famous Comedy Store, sharing the same stage with legends such as Richard Pryor, Eddie Murphy, Gary Shandling, Robin Williams, Andrew Dice Clay & Jim Carrey to name a few, in what would be an early master class by the best comedic talents of our times.

That his first professional role in "Sneakers" would bring him face to face with the actual Sundance Kid, Robert Redford was a beautiful irony and along with fellow Oscar winners, Sir Ben Kingsley, Sidney Poitier & cast members Dan Aykroyd, River Phoenix and James Earl Jones, was a sign that he was on the right path.

Jo continued training in Los Angeles with renowned acting coaches Howard Fine & Charlie Laughton, Ernie Lively and in New York, Joanne Gibson & Susan Scanlon along with writing several screenplays which lead to writing & directing the short "Who's Killing the Meter Maids?" Starring Mariska Hargitay & Richard Steinmetz as a duo trying to solve the serial killing of meter maids. This film inspired Jo to establish Nichol Moon Entertainment & Arrival Entertainment, Production Service Companies helping indie filmmakers realize their dreams & consulted on over 250 productions including, features such as Doug Liman's "Swingers", shorts, music videos, PSA's, etc. To claim that Jo & Company enabled the independent film movement of the 90's is an under-statement. Jo went on to win "Best Feature" at the 1999 New York Film & Video festival for the film 'Blink of an Eye'.

In 2006 Jo co-founded Film Tiger to produce independent feature films Timber Falls, Night Train and Stag Night. Inspired by his brother's relationship with his daughter, Jo wrote, produced and directed "Going Thru A Thing" about a small time criminal who coaches his daughter's basketball team for all the wrong reasons.

Subsequently Jo went on to co-write and produce Battle Drone about the future of warfare, as well as producing duties on Frat Pack, Billionaire (Best Comedy Feature, Burbank Intl Film Festival) Escape the Field & The Doorman, starring Ruby Rose and Jean Reno.

Jo continues to write, produce and direct, seeking out material and creatives who love the craft and love people even more. Fortunate to be in an industry that is constantly changing, inspiring and challenging Jo remains grateful for the opportunities and freedoms afforded by the "best job in the world"

White Flags is Jo's first book and has taken several years to complete. The journey of "White Flags" began as a feature film screenplay and subsequently was adapted into a book for the ability to tell a deeper more meaningful story.

Jo continues to write books and screenplays, produces and directs and enjoys the freedom of traveling to experience stories and perspectives from around the world.

www.ingramcontent.com/pod-product-compliance
Lightning Source LLC
Chambersburg PA
CBHW072005210726
48294CB00013B/1483